Exit Strategy

ALSO BY MARTHA WELLS

THE MURDERBOT DIARIES
All Systems Red
Artificial Condition
Rogue Protocol

BOOKS OF THE RAKSURA
The Cloud Roads
The Serpent Sea
The Siren Depths
The Edge of Worlds
The Harbors of the Sun
Stories of the Raksura: Volume I (short fiction)
Stories of the Raksura: Volume II (short fiction)

THE FALL OF ILE-RIEN TRILOGY
The Wizard Hunters
The Ships of Air
The Gate of Gods

STANDALONE ILE-RIEN BOOKS
The Element of Fire
The Death of the Necromancer
Between Worlds: The Collected Ile-Rien and Cineth Stories

YA NOVELS
Emilie and the Hollow World
Emilie and the Sky World
Blade Singer (with Aaron de Orive)

TIE-IN NOVELS
Stargate Atlantis: Reliquary
Stargate Atlantis: Entanglement
Star Wars: Razor's Edge

City of Bones
Wheel of the Infinite

EXIT STRATEGY

THE MURDERBOT DIARIES

MARTHA WELLS

A TOM DOHERTY ASSOCIATES BOOK

NEW YORK

This is a work of fiction. All of the characters, organizations, and events portrayed in this novella are either products of the author's imagination or are used fictitiously.

EXIT STRATEGY

Copyright © 2018 by Martha Wells

All rights reserved.

Edited by Lee Harris

A Tor.com Book
Published by Tom Doherty Associates
175 Fifth Avenue
New York, NY 10010

www.tor.com

Tor® is a registered trademark of Macmillan Publishing Group, LLC.

The Library of Congress Cataloging-in-Publication Data
is available upon request.

ISBN 978-1-250-19185-4 (hardcover)
ISBN 978-1-250-18546-4 (ebook)

Our books may be purchased in bulk for promotional, educational, or business use. Please contact your local bookseller or the Macmillan Corporate and Premium Sales Department at 1-800-221-7945, extension 5442, or by email at MacmillanSpecialMarkets@macmillan.com.

First Edition: October 2018

Printed in the United States of America

16 15 14

Exit Strategy

Chapter One

WHEN I GOT BACK to HaveRatton Station, a bunch of humans tried to kill me. Considering how much I'd been thinking about killing a bunch of humans, it was only fair.

Ship was on approach and I was waiting impatiently to pick up HaveRatton's feed. Since Ship was a minimum capacity bot pilot and had all the brains and personality of a heat shield generator, I was also monitoring all its inputs and caught the navigation alert when it came in. (I knew Ship wouldn't betray me intentionally, but the chance of it doing so unintentionally was resting at a solid 84 percent.)

The alert was from HaveRatton's Port Authority, and ordered Ship to divert away from its usual slot in the private commercial docks to another section at the end of the public passenger embarkation zone.

I still had the schematic of HaveRatton from when I had boarded Ship here on the way to Milu. I could see that section of the embarkation zone was right next to the

PA's docks, where the deployment point for the station's security response team was.

Oh, that's not suspicious at all.

Was it about me? Maybe, probably? Ship had carried Wilken and Gerth, who had been sent to sabotage GoodNightLander Independent's attempt to reclaim GrayCris' abandoned terraforming facility, so it might be about them. Wilken and/or Gerth were hopefully being held by GI somewhere now, and GI might have requested HaveRatton do a routine search for evidence.

It didn't matter. If there was anybody waiting for Ship, I couldn't be aboard when it docked.

I could direct Ship to a different dock but that wasn't a great idea. The PA would not only know someone aboard had done it, but that that someone was riding a bot-piloted cargo transport whose feed manifest said it was currently traveling without crew or passengers and was on minimal life-support. Even stations as big and heavily armed as HaveRatton had to be careful of anomalous approaches that might turn out to be raiders attempting to board. (It would be a stupid attempt, since Ship couldn't carry enough raiders to do anything but die messily in the embarkation zone, but I'd spent my entire life on security contracts trying to stop humans from similar catastrophic stupidity.) It might worry the station command enough that they would fire on Ship. Ship might be unresponsive but it was doing its best and I didn't want it hurt.

So it was a good thing I still had the evac suit.

I'd used it to escape Abene's shuttle after the combat bot attack—another thing that had happened that I wished I could delete from my memory. (Deleting memories like that doesn't work. I can delete things from my data storage, but not from the organic parts of my head. The company had purged my memory a few times, including my whole mass murder incident, and the images hung around like ghosts in an endless historical family drama serial.)

(I like endless historical family drama serials, but in real life, ghosts are way more annoying.)

Earlier when I was getting ready for station arrival, I had packed the evac suit into a supply locker. I figured since Ship seldom ran passengers along with cargo, it would be a long time before somebody finally noticed it wasn't on inventory and actually checked its docs and registrations. Now I started unpacking it, fast.

I really didn't want to get caught.

I stuffed my bag under my jacket and got the suit on and activated. As Ship made its docking maneuver and eased up on the designated slot, I cycled through the cargo module airlock on the opposite side. Ship's drones gathered to watch me, confused as to why I was going out the wrong door and beeping sadly about it. As Ship locked on to the station, I slipped out the airlock and sent a close and seal request. As I pulled myself along Ship's outer skin, I deleted the last few bits of me from its memory.

Bye, Ship. You were there when it counted.

If a report of what had happened on Milu had gone out on a faster transport (Ship's progress was leisurely at best) then it could have easily beat me here. They might know that a SecUnit had come to Milu, saved some humans, failed to save a human form bot, killed the shit out of three combat bots, and that Ship was the only transport who had left Milu right after all that happened.

Me not being aboard when they searched, with no sign of having been there, would obscure the issue somewhat. It's not like I needed any food or used waste disposal. I'd used a little extra air and the shower but I'd purged the recycling logs. A forensic sweep might show that I'd been there. If forensic sweeps worked like they did in the entertainment media, which, come to think about it, I had no idea if they did or not.

(Note to self: look up real forensic sweeps.)

I reached the side of the station, doing a physical scan for security cams or drones or whatever while searching for feed and comm signals. Other ships were locked on nearby, but all I could see were hulls and bulky cargo modules, no large viewports with humans looking out wondering who that random escaping SecUnit in the suit was. I caught a few signals, but all were either debris detectors or cargo bot guides. I followed the line of magnetic clamps used by the cargo bots to secure modules to the station, and found a bot in the process of removing a module from a large cargo transport. I accessed the bot's feed channel and checked its work orders. The transport it was currently working on was bot-piloted, crew on leave, passengers disembarked. I asked the cargo bot if I could go inside the transport before it inserted the new empty module. It said sure.

(Humans never think to tell their bots things like, say, don't respond to random individuals wandering the outside of the station. Bots are instructed to report and repel theft attempts, but no one ever tells them not to answer polite requests from other bots.)

I climbed inside the empty module structure and up to the airlock. I pinged the transport, it pinged back. I didn't have time to bribe it, so I sent it the official station hauler's security key I had just pulled from the cargo bot's memory, and asked it if I could come inside and walk through and out to the dock. It said sure.

I cycled through the lock, took off the evac suit, and found a storage locker to pack it into. At the main airlock, I borrowed the security camera to take a look at myself.

I'd removed the blood and fluid from my clothes back on Ship, in the cleaning unit in its passenger restroom, but there hadn't been anything on board to fix the projectile and shrapnel holes. Fortunately the jacket I was wearing was dark and the holes weren't that visible, and the shirt collar was just high enough to cover the disabled data port in the back of my neck.

Normally that wasn't a problem, as most humans had never seen a SecUnit without armor and would assume the port was just an augment. If the humans who had diverted Ship were after me, they probably knew that a SecUnit without armor would look like an augmented human.

(Possibly I was overthinking this. I do that; it's the anxiety that comes with being a part-organic murderbot. The upside was paranoid attention to detail. The downside was also paranoid attention to detail.)

I made sure I was running the code I'd written to make my walking gait and body language more human, deleted myself out of the transport's log, and walked out through the main airlock into the station docks.

I was already in the feed, using it to hack into the station's weapons-scanning drones, telling them to ignore me. It was always important to hack the weapon scanners, since I have two inbuilt energy weapons in my forearms. This time it was more important, because among other things I had an armor-piercing projectile weapon and ammo in my bag.

It was one of Wilken and Gerth's weapons that I'd taken when I left Milu. I'd spent some time on the return trip using Ship's tool suite to take it apart and rebuild it into a more compact form, so it was easier to conceal. So now I was not only a rogue unit, I was a rogue unit carrying a weapon designed to shoot armored security. Which is just playing to the humans' expectations, I guess.

But fooling the weapons scanners was so much easier now than it had been the first time I'd done it while leaving Port FreeCommerce. Part of it was learning the quirks of the different security systems I was encountering. But what really helped was that all this coding and working with different systems on the fly had opened up some new neural pathways and processing space. I'd noticed it on Milu, when I'd been handling multiple inputs without any Hub or SecSystem assistance, to the point where I thought my brain was going to implode. Hard work really did make you improve; who knew?

Following my map, I left the secure (supposedly secure) dock area and took the walkway toward the station mall. It passed over the end of the public embarkation zone and the PA dock where Ship had been directed.

I had been in crowds of humans enough times by now I shouldn't panic anymore—I had ridden on a transport with a whole crowd of humans who thought I was an augmented human security consultant and talked at me nonstop nearly the whole time. Except there was a little panic.

I should be over this by now.

Every nerve in the organic parts of me twitched as I blended with a large group of transport passengers. It helps that in stations like this, humans and augmented humans are distracted. Everybody's a stranger, everybody's checking the feed for info or communication or entertainment while they're walking. As the walkway passed in front of Ship's slot, I spotted a big group down on the embarkation floor. With the rest of the crowd of humans, I turned my head to glance down.

Twenty-three of them in power suits, all heavily armed, forming up for a boarding operation. None were in SecUnit armor, and I wasn't picking up any pings, so they were probably all human or augmented human. Forty-seven security drones of various sizes and armament circled over their heads in a deployment-ready swarm. I caught a station security drone and had it zoom in on the shoulder logo of a suit. I didn't recognize it immediately, except for the fact that it wasn't a HaveRatton station logo. I tagged it for a future image search.

HaveRatton Station Security was there, but they were back at the entrance to the Port Authority zone, watching the boarding operation. So whoever it was had contracted with HaveRatton to bring an armed team in. That's expensive. And worrying. You don't need twenty-three humans in power suits and a flotilla of security drones for an evidence search.

Station security had to be using their drones to keep an eye on the security company stamping around on their dock area. I checked my captive StationSec drone's recording buffer and found nearly an hour of intercepted comm traffic. I downloaded it and ran a query for the word SecUnit. It hit almost immediately.

SecUnit. You think this thing is really onboard?
Intel says possibly. I—
With its controller?
No controller, dim-iot, that's why they call them rogues.
Oh yeah. It was about me.

On Milu's terraforming facility/illegal alien remnant mining platform, Wilken and Gerth had recognized me as a SecUnit. It had come in handy at the time, but it wasn't something I wanted to happen again.

Ever again.

My friend ART had changed my configuration, removing up to a centimeter from my arms and legs so I wouldn't match a scan for SecUnit standard body shape. ART's alterations to my code had made parts of me grow sparse, soft, humanlike body hair, and changed the way my skin met the edges of my inorganic parts, so they looked more like augments. It was subtle, something ART thought would lessen human suspicion on a subliminal level. (ART's pretentious like that.) The change in code had also made my eyebrows and the hair on my head get thicker, and that made my face look far more different than such a slight change should. I didn't like it, but it was necessary.

But it wasn't enough of a change to fool humans familiar with SecUnits. (Granted, running up a wall in front of Wilken and Gerth had been a dead giveaway before they even got a real look at me.) I could control my behavior (well, sort of, mostly) but I needed to control my appearance.

So while I was still on Ship, I had used ART's templates to alter my code temporarily to let the hair on my head grow at an accelerated rate. (Accelerated because if I screwed up and started getting near the bipedal furry media monster end of the spectrum, I'd still have a chance to fix it.) I gave the hair on my head another two centimeters of growth, then stopped it when I hit my target.

To check my results, I'd pulled up an image from my archived video, and found a good view of my face from Dr. Mensah's camera. I don't usually use cameras to look at myself because why the hell would I want to do that, but I had been on contract then and still collecting all my clients' feeds. From the timestamp, the image was from when we'd been standing outside the hoppers, when GrayCris was hunting us, and she had asked me to let the others see my face so they would trust me.

I'd compared that old image with my current image via drone cam. After all the changes, I did look different now, and more human.

I didn't like it even more.

But now that I was back on HaveRatton with an as yet unidentified security force looking for me, it was coming in handy. The next step was to get rid of my clothing and its obvious projectile holes. At the edge of the station mall, I forced myself to walk into one of the big travelers' supply places.

I had used station vending machines to buy memory clips, but I had never been in an actual shop before. Even though the vending was all automated, and I sort of knew what to do based on what I had seen on the entertainment feed, it was still weird. (And by weird I mean an agonizing level of anxiety.) Fortunately there are apparently humans as clueless as I was because as soon as I crossed the threshold the shop's feed immediately sent me an interactive instruction module.

It guided me to one of the empty vending booths, which was completely enclosed. Telling it to shut the privacy door was such a relief my performance reliability percentage went up half a point. The booth scanned my hard currency card and then offered a set of menus.

I picked the one that was labeled as basic, practical, and comfortable for travel. I hesitated over long skirts, wide pants, full-length caftans, and tunics and jackets that went to the knees. The idea of combining them all, and having a lot of clothing as a buffer between me and the outside world, was attractive, but I wasn't used to it and I was afraid that would show. (It had taken me long enough to figure out what to do with my arms and hands while walking and standing still; extra clothing meant that much more potential for attention-drawing mistakes.) The scarves and hats and other head and face coverings, some of which had human cultural functions, were also tempting, but it was exactly the kind of thing a SecUnit trying to hide might use, and would just flag me for additional security scans.

I'd worn two different sets of human clothes by now, so I had a better idea of what was most efficient for me. I picked workboots not much different from the ones I'd stolen back on Port FreeCommerce, self-sizing and with some shielding to protect against heavy things dropping on them, not as important for me as a human. Then pants with lots of sealable pockets, a long-sleeved shirt with a collar to cover my data port, and another soft hooded jacket. Okay, so it was extremely similar to what I had been wearing, just in a different arrangement of black and dark blue. I authorized the payment, and the packets dropped out of the slot.

When I put the new clothes on, I had a strange feeling I usually associated with finding a new show on the entertainment feed that looked good. I "liked" these clothes. Maybe I actually liked them enough to remove the quotation marks around "liked." I don't like things in general that can't be downloaded via the entertainment feed.

Maybe because I'd picked them myself.

Maybe.

I got a replacement knapsack, too, a better one with more sealable pockets. I dressed, got a discount because I was willing to dump my old clothes into the shop's recycler, and left the booth.

Back out in the station mall, blending with the crowd, I started downloading new entertainment media and transport schedules, and started a feed search for news reports. My image search had turned up a name for the security company logo: Palisade. I started a search on it, too.

I needed to get off HaveRatton as soon as possible, and figure out a good way to get my memory clips to Dr. Mensah.

The clips I had stashed in my arm had a lot of data drawn directly from the Milu diggers about the strange synthetics that GrayCris had illegally extracted under the guise of a terraforming operation. And the memory clip I had found in Wilken and Gerth's gear was even more revealing. It was records of their work history for GrayCris, carefully organized and arranged, ready to submit to journalists or a corporate rival. I think it was a blackmail threat, or an attempt to ensure that GrayCris didn't try to kill them. Whatever it was, I had it now.

Taking it and the other clips to Mensah in person would be the most secure method, and that's what I meant to do. I just wasn't sure I wanted to see her again. (Or more accurately, for her to see me again.)

Thinking about her brought up a whole knot of confused emotion I didn't want to deal with right now. Or ever, actually. But it wasn't a decision I had to make immediately. (Yeah, "Or ever, actually" applied there, too.) I could always break in to wherever she was staying and leave the clips in her belongings with a note. (I'd thought a lot about the note. I had other options but would probably go with "Hope this evidence against GrayCris helps, signed Murderbot.") I needed to concentrate on how to find out if she was still on Port FreeCommerce or had gone back to the Preservation Alliance without—

My newsfeed search turned up a string of hits and the tagline on the top-ranked most-popular made me stop in my tracks. Luckily I was in a wide place in the mall, where the big transport lines had their offices, and the sparse crowd spread out and flowed around me. I made myself move over to the nearest office entrance, and stood in the spot where their proprietary feed was displaying advertising and informational vids. It wasn't ideal, but I had to be somewhere where I could stand still and just concentrate on the news story.

Dr. Mensah had been accused by GrayCris of corporate espionage.

How the hell had we gotten to that point from the last newsburst I'd picked up here? There had been multiple lawsuits in play, but GrayCris had clearly been the aggressor in the violence against the survey teams. Besides all the other evidence, we had my feed recording and Mensah's suit camera video of GrayCris representatives admitting guilt. Not even the cheap stupid half-assed bond company that had owned me could fuck that up.

Except apparently it could. And Dr. Mensah was a planetary leader from a non-corporate political entity; how could she be charged with corporate espionage? I mean, I don't know anything about it because we never got education modules on human law stuff, but it sounded wrong.

I got past my initial outrage and managed to read the rest of the newsburst. GrayCris had made the charge, but nobody knew if they had brought an actual litigation (counterlitigation? Was that a word?) or not. It was all speculation because the journalists couldn't find Mensah.

Wait, what?

So where was she? Where were the others? Had they gone back to Preservation and left her alone? From what I'd been able to research, Preservation's attitude to its planetary leaders was extremely casual. At home, Dr. Mensah didn't even need security. But it was stupid to leave her alone on Port FreeCommerce where anything could happen to her. Had happened to her.

I wanted to put my fist through the nearest corporate logo. Idiotic humans don't understand how to be safe, idiotic humans thought every place was like stupid boring Preservation!

I needed more info; obviously I'd missed some important developments. I worked my way back up the news timeline, searching the related tags, doing it thoroughly, trying not to panic. According to records that Port FreeCommerce had made available to get the journalists off its back, Arada, Overse, Bharadwaj, and Volescu had all left for Preservation about thirty cycles ago. Mensah was supposed to follow with the others, but hadn't. So far so good.

The next data point was buried in another story so deeply even I almost missed it. There had been a news release by GrayCris that Mensah had gone to TranRollinHyfa to answer their litigation, but Port FreeCommerce couldn't confirm.

Where the fuck was TranRollinHyfa?

A frantic search on the public feed information bases told me TranRollinHyfa was a station, a major hub, where close to two hundred companies, including GrayCris, had their corporate headquarters. So, not exclusively enemy territory. Funny how that didn't make me feel any better.

The next relevant newsburst speculated that Mensah had gone to TranRollinHyfa to pursue testimony on behalf of Preservation and DeltFall in the suit against GrayCris. The newsburst after that speculated that she was going to testify in GrayCris' possibly apocryphal suit against her. Terrifyingly, the two entities that might actually know anything, the Preservation Alliance and my stupid half-assed ex-owner bond company on Port FreeCommerce, had made no official statement except to say she was definitely on TranRollinHyfa.

Mensah wasn't stupid, she would never have gone near hostile corporate territory without protection. If she had gone to TranRollinHyfa voluntarily, the bond for a trip to visit GrayCris, who had already tried to kill her once, would be expensive to buy and more expensive to execute, and the company would have to agree to anything to get her out, including sending gunships. Safer and therefore cheaper to stay on Port FreeCommerce, the bond company's major deployment center, and make all the parties with testimony come there. That's what the company would have insisted on.

Conclusion: Mensah hadn't gone to TranRollinHyfa voluntarily.

Somebody had tricked, trapped, or forced her to go. But why? If GrayCris was going to do that, why wait so long, why give all the witnesses involved time to bring their suits and testify and give their evidence to journalists? What had happened that had panicked GrayCris so much that . . .

Oh. Oh, shit.

Chapter Two

I NEEDED TO GO, and go fast. And not on a bot-piloted transport. Not finding me on Ship would throw off Palisade's pursuit, but not for long, and if they had any brains at all they would be checking automated transports. I pulled schedules for extra-fast crewed passenger transports (No, not a direct trip. I'm apparently an idiot, but not that big an idiot.) and found one leaving in four hours heading for a major hub. From there, I could get where I needed to go.

I hadn't traveled like this before, mainly because I hadn't wanted to. At first, I'd doubted my ability to hack weapons scanners while I was hacking the ID and payment systems. But now I had no excuse not to, thanks to Wilken and Gerth.

I had ended up with their emergency go-bag, filled with hard currency cards and a variety of ID markers. The markers are meant for subcutaneous insertion and contain identifying information. Normally they wouldn't be readable by anything but the scanners designed for the purpose, but with a little fine-tuning my scan had been able to view the encoded data, and I had examined them all on the trip back to HaveRatton.

Identity markers in the Corporation Rim usually had a lot of information on the bearer, but these were temporaries meant for travelers from outside the Rim. They had a string of numbers from a non-corporate political entity authorizing travel, place of origin, and a name. Obviously this was why Wilken and Gerth had them, so they could switch identities at need. Corporate political entities are more interested in keeping track of their own humans than anybody else's. I had seen on the media that travel was easier for non-citizens inside the Corporation Rim than citizens, sub-citizens, and all the other categories each different political entity had to keep track of their humans. (It could be worse. At least humans could cut out their ID markers; I had corporate logos etched onto parts of me I couldn't get rid of.)

I went to a public rest area, paid for an enclosed cubicle with the hard currency card, and picked an ID with the name Jian from Parthalos Absalo. I peeled back the skin around my shoulder joint and inserted the marker under it. I had to dial down my pain receptors in that area, but there was no inconvenient leaking.

I'd been pretending to be human off and on since I left

Dr. Mensah, but this was the first time I'd had anything on me that officially labeled me as human. It was weird.

I didn't like it.

I paid for passage at a kiosk at the edge of the embarkation zone and had my new ID scanned there and at the transport's lock when I entered. I had to hack two weapons scans, and adjust the personal scan results at the lock to show a less excessive number of augments. I'd paid for a private cabin with an attached restroom facility and automated meal delivery. (I didn't need the meals but it would give me something to dump in the waste recycler so the levels wouldn't look off to anyone who checked.) The ship's feed led me to the cabin and I saw only four humans in the corridor and heard five others as I passed a lounge. My goal was to not see them again the rest of the seven-cycle trip.

The cabin was nicer than the one I'd had on my only other passenger transport. It had a bunk with a bedding packet and a small display surface, a door leading to the tiny restroom facility, a storage cabinet for personal possessions, and a meal distribution receptacle. I sealed the door, didn't bother to sit down or even drop my bag.

I had feed searches to do while we were still attached to station.

I set one for TranRollinHyfa and expanded my newsburst searches with new keywords and time limits. I had already grabbed new media downloads on my walk to the embarkation zone. I knew I was going to need the distraction.

I thought I knew at least part of what was going on, and it wasn't good. From GrayCris' perspective, these things had happened in sequence:

1) Dr. Mensah had bought a (used, somewhat battered) SecUnit, which had then disappeared, no one knew where. 2) Dr. Mensah had said, in an interview sent out in newsbursts carried by transports all across the Corporation Rim, that someone needed to investigate Milu because GrayCris abandoning a terraforming facility was suspicious. (Never mind that the journalist had brought up Milu, not her.) 3) A SecUnit had shown up on Milu and helped an assessment team contracted by GoodNightLander Independent to a) save the facility from falling into the planet, and b) acquire proof that it was an illegal mining operation and not a terraforming facility at all.

The news of 3a and 3b was already in newsbursts making their way through the Corporation Rim, along with Abene and the others' eyewitness accounts and Wilken and Gerth's testimony about who had hired them.

Obviously, GrayCris thought Mensah had sent me to Milu to fuck them over.

Oops.

This was a stressful trip, right up there with the one where ART introduced itself to me by implying that it might delete my brain and the one where I kept thinking about Miki. And the one with Ayres and the other humans who had sold themselves into contract slavery.

I guess most of my trips so far had been this stressful.

This time it was anxiety, and I did what I always do, which is watch media. One of the new shows I'd downloaded randomly at HaveRatton turned out to be a long historical drama about early human exploration in space. It was listed as a fictionalized documentary (I'm not sure what that means, either) but there were attached sidebars throughout with info about the real history, which were supposedly accurate. It was odd to see that there had been a variation of SecUnits back then. They didn't use cloned human parts, but actual human parts from humans who had catastrophic injuries or illnesses, and had decided to have their parts used for what they called Augmented Rovers. Some of the humans in the primary story line had actually known one of the ARs when it was a human, and they were all still friends. The ARs weren't human-form, but got to choose their assignments and which humans they worked with. They talked back and forth with the humans, gave advice, sometimes led rescue parties, and saved the day a lot. Despite all the convincingly informative sidebars, I had trouble believing it was true. I stopped in the middle of the second episode and switched to a musical comedy.

Anyway, there was a difference in watching media because I was safe on a transport with no one making me do anything, and watching media because I was trying not to think about all the ways I'd screwed up and what might happen next, a future that was bound to include even more creative screw-ups on my part. I had gotten used to the former and I hated going back to the latter.

I did try to prepare. I pulled everything the transport's feed had on TranRollinHyfa, which wasn't much more than an updated version of the standard tourist packet that I had already downloaded from HaveRatton, but it did give me the names of a lot of the corporations that had bases or headquarters there.

The security company Palisade had a large office there. Why was that not a surprise?

I also did a lot of work on my code for beating security cameras. I had developed it on RaviHyral right before almost getting my client Tapan killed. It was a method for deleting me from the camera's recording and replacing me with images before and after I walked past. It wasn't perfect, and I worked on making it better, adding code to work with different types and brands of SecSystems, and a greater number of cameras and angles.

When we came through the wormhole, I was just glad the first leg of the trip was over.

Nobody was waiting for me when we docked at the transit hub so at least that told me that Wilken and Gerth's IDs were good. I only spent ten hours there, all of it in a tiny room in a transient hostel. I downloaded some new shows, but I spent most of the time pulling files from information bases for anything on TranRollinHyfa. This took longer since most of the bases I needed access to were proprietary corporate ones and I had to hack my way in before I could even tell if they had what I was looking for or not. I also ran my usual searches on newsbursts. (Nothing new on Mensah except lots of speculation that didn't help my anxiety level.)

When it was almost time to go, I traded out the Jian ID for one with the name Kiran. I had contemplated one more obfuscating hop, but I didn't know what was happening with Mensah and the thought that I might already be too late wasn't helpful. So I booked a passage on another fast passenger transport direct to TranRollinHyfa.

I hesitated over my memory clips from Milu, the ones

still hidden in my arm and Wilken and Gerth's clip. I didn't know how useful the information was anymore.

But Miki had died for that information, whether it knew it or not.

Taking it into GrayCris territory with me would be stupid. In the transient room, I removed the clips from my arm, then left for the embarkation zone. On the way, I stopped at a shipping kiosk and bought a small parcel package. I rolled the clips up in the protective wrapper, included Wilken and Gerth's clip, and sealed the container. I addressed it to all of Dr. Mensah's marital partners on their farm on Preservation. (I had all the info for the shipping form, lying around in longterm memory storage, from my old company's records of PreservationAux. Wow, that seemed like a long time ago.)

I'd boarded my next passenger transport and was hiding in my private cabin when I caught a new newsburst, relayed from a ship that had just come in to dock. It was a brief statement from the Preservation Alliance by Dr. Bharadwaj.

It was unexpectedly odd to see a familiar human, even if she looked really angry. All she said was that Preservation was "taking steps" to resolve the issues with GrayCris.

Huh. I lay down on the bunk and stared at the metal

ceiling. There was a background buzz of traffic in the ship's public feed as the docking clamps were released. I was monitoring the private activity to make sure no one was chatting about the SecUnit hiding in a passenger cabin incompetently pretending to be human. I replayed Bharadwaj's statement seven times.

I might be wrong. I knew interpreting the emotional subtext in the speech and appearance of real humans was completely different from interpreting it in shows and serials. (For one thing, the shows and serials were trying to communicate accurately with the viewer. As far as I could tell, real humans usually didn't know what the hell they were doing.) But the interpretation I wanted to make of Bharadwaj's vid statement was that Mensah was being held by GrayCris, who had threatened her life if Preservation didn't make a formal statement at least implying that they were in amicable negotiations to settle with GrayCris.

I looked back over the newsburst that had accompanied it and found there was still no statement by DeltFall, whose survey team GrayCris had slaughtered. Or my ex-owner the company, which was probably torn between fury and shitting itself over the amount of equipment and bond payments lost in the debacle and desperate to have someone pay for it. I mean, literally pay for it.

GrayCris could buy the company off for a big enough credit payout but so far it hadn't done that. But maybe GrayCris couldn't afford that payout.

GrayCris had done all this to acquire strange synthetics, alien remnants. Now that everybody knew that, they couldn't sell them, or develop them, or whatever they had been planning to do with them. It meant they were desperate, too.

That wasn't good.

After four cycles by ship's local time, the passenger transport came through the wormhole and I picked up the edge of the TranRollinHyfa Station feed.

It looked bigger up close. The station itself was larger than Port FreeCommerce, with three interconnected transit rings below the main hull. Usually the transit ring circles the station, with the main part where humans and augmented humans live or do whatever in the center. Or, I guess, I've never been in those parts except for the deployment center on Port FreeCommerce, which was near the transit ring.

I picked up the feed but it was crammed with advertising, with the transit schedules and service listings swamped by corporation ads that were dissolving into static because other corporations had paid fees to drown them out. Well, that was all useless. I dropped it and picked up the ship's comm, which was monitoring the Port Authority's feed. There were still ads, but at least the PA was able to get a word in edgewise every now and then. One of those words was a navigation alert and—

Huh.

I pulled it up on the transport's feed, where the scan and nav was running for the crew. There was a company gunship hanging off the station.

Not on approach, not waiting for a docking slot. Just maintaining position.

There was no mistake about who owned it, the navigation alert included the stupid logo the gunship was broadcasting in its otherwise blocked feed, the same logo etched into my non-organic parts. I checked the alert's timestamp. Converted to my local time it equaled twenty cycles, give or take.

It could have been here for another contract, but that seemed like a big coincidence. Gunships don't have any other purpose except to go fast and blow stuff up, and contracts for them are tricky, because of the treaties between corporate and non-corporate political entities.

I had thought that if Mensah had actually gone to TranRollinHyfa voluntarily to negotiate with GrayCris, then the bond might have been high enough to require a gunship. But then why wasn't it docked? Did Mensah need rescuing or what? I needed intel, and there was one way to get it.

The station approach traffic was heavy, and we were showing a twenty-seven-minute docking delay. Twenty-seven minutes was more than enough time for me to do something stupid.

I sank into the ship's comm. The approach protocol the PA had managed to slip out between ads stipulated that comms be set to monitor all signal traffic, voice and feed. This was so ships could bypass the choked station feed and pick up any alerts or alarms the other ships might broadcast.

It was harder to sort and separate them without the comm system assisting but I knew what I was looking for. After six minutes I found it: the company gunship's encrypted feed, twined around its comm signal like the melody in a music sample. I pulled the feed in and applied the key, and—this could be a mistake, did I need intel this badly? Yeah, yeah, I did. I needed to know if Mensah was here on a mission or under duress—I sent the gunship's bot pilot a ping and added the code that would tell it I was in stealth mode.

It acknowledged. It recognized me as also company property, since I had the decryption key and I was using the right salutation. I didn't think it would notify its crew that it had been contacted by what it had every reason to identify as another company bot, not unless someone had told it to. Another SecUnit would have reported me immediately, but then a SecUnit would have known what I was and that I shouldn't be out here.

I waited, listening in to make sure no one had noticed the offsite connection. No alarms were raised. I could tell feed traffic aboard the ship was light, and mostly in standby mode. They were waiting for something.

I mentally braced myself and sent the bot pilot *Status: update (stealth)*. After a long three seconds, it returned a databurst. I sent an acknowledgment and broke free of the connection.

I focused on the ceiling of the cabin again. If I was lucky, nobody would check the bot pilot's contact log. The company had been paid for me and taken me off inventory, but I had no legal status in corporate territory without Mensah. If they realized I was here, they could report me to station authorities, or decide to catch me and forcibly separate me into my component parts, or anything in between.

I checked the databurst for tracers and malware and then unpacked it.

Well, this was ... potentially a disaster. Shortly after the gunship had arrived at TranRollinHyfa, the contract status had gone from *Retrieve: Active* to *Retrieve: Suspended*

Due to Neutral Party Access Denial, Escalation Out of Contracted Parameters. That meant that the gunship had been sent to retrieve an endangered client, but the operation had been halted because the retrieval had been blocked, and by something other than just being beyond the range of the client's ability to pay. The client ID code was Mensah's, the same one from my contract, which meant this was an extension of her original safety bond for the planetary survey. Which, okay, I didn't know it worked like that, but it was confirmation Mensah was here, or at least that the company's current intel thought she was here.

And the fucking gunship was sitting out here not doing anything about it. I'm guessing GrayCris had somehow gotten TranRollinHyfa to refuse docking and operational permission, meaning the company couldn't land its armed retrieval team without fighting TRH station security and the company hadn't been paid enough to do that.

The other code in the status was *Secondary Clients Status: Recognizance.* That was almost worse—it meant someone else named in the bond (probably Pin-Lee, Ratthi, or Gurathin, since they hadn't been listed in the newsburst as returning to Preservation) had left company protection and were in the wind. There was only one way to be in the wind between a gunship and an armed station: they must have taken a shuttle, certified themselves as unarmed to get past the operational prohibition, and been allowed to dock.

So that was four of them I had to worry about.

Waiting was stressful, and I watched an episode of my favorite, *The Rise and Fall of Sanctuary Moon*, while the transport finished its approach and went through docking procedures. Then the ship's feed signaled that it was time to disembark.

One reason I'd picked this particular fast non-bot-piloted transport out of the others heading here was because there were 127 passengers, forty-three of whom were traveling together. They didn't disappoint me and disembarked in a single noisy confused mob. I walked out surrounded by them and was across the embarkation floor and up into the transparent pipe of the elevated walkway before they became distracted by the vending and advertising bays and started to thin out. I kept walking.

By that point I'd deflected three weapons scans and had hacked the restricted feeds for the various drone security cameras. The security was tighter for disembarking passengers than the other transit rings and stations

I'd visited. Unusually tight for a station that sold its public feed for ads that drowned out the safety info and official announcements. (You could tell which humans and augmented humans were trying to use its mapping function because they kept walking up to blocked exits and walls.)

I had also been hit by at least four different recognition scans. These scans are usually searching for known humans or augmented humans that the station security is keeping tabs on, not random escaped SecUnits. (Random escaped SecUnits is not nearly as prevalent a problem as the entertainment feed would have you believe.) But I was glad I'd listened to ART and let it change my configuration. I was glad for every single precaution I'd taken, even the ones that had seemed paranoid at the time.

I didn't spot any armed security patrols but there were extra drones, small ones, a different brand and configuration than the ones I was used to. After I modified my queries to block the stupid ads, I got a download and search of the news feed started, as well as the port's public dock assignment list. I checked the port map that had managed to fight its way through the advertising chaff, and took the walkway heading up into the station mall.

My transport had docked on the second transit ring, so there were a lot of ramps to walk up, if you didn't want to take the lift pods, which I didn't. I wasn't catching pings, but a check of the station directory showed two security companies based here who had SecUnits available for rental, EinoArzu and Stockade Kumaran. Palisade was listed as a security company, but not as a company that supplied SecUnits. That didn't necessarily mean they didn't have them, it just meant they didn't advertise them.

I wasn't too worried about SecUnits being used against me at this point. SecUnits would be able to identify me as a rogue unit on sight (or on ping, more accurately) but we were never used on transit rings. The security companies would ship us (them) through the port as cargo, to keep from panicking the humans. I mean, there's a first time for everything, but it just wasn't likely, maybe a fifteen percent chance at best.

Even if they did deploy, they still had to find me. The governor modules wouldn't let the SecUnits hack systems or search for my hacks, not on their own without human direction. (And I didn't think GrayCris had any idea how much hacking I was responsible for.) Only combat SecUnits could detect or counteract my hacks without a human supervisor.

Still, my human skin was prickling with nerves. The extra security seemed to support a theory I had. Or maybe I mean a hypothesis. Whatever, the idea was that if Bharadwaj's statement in the newsburst had been a message to GrayCris, a sign that Preservation would cooperate to save Dr. Mensah, then the stories about Mensah being arrested, about her going to or somehow being taken to TranRollinHyfa were messages, too. Messages to me.

GrayCris thought the newsbursts were how Mensah had ordered me to go to Milu, so it stood to reason they would use newsbursts to lure me here.

It wasn't a great theory/hypothesis. They had Mensah, so I don't know why they would want me. They knew I'd been on Milu, did they suspect I had left with an armful of incriminating data? But GoodNightLander Independent had Milu now and would hopefully be mad enough to look for incriminating data of their own, so they could publicly complain about it on their own newsfeeds. GrayCris going after me and Mensah wasn't going to stop that.

But they were humans—who knows why they did anything?

It made it all the more obvious that now that I'd gotten in here, I needed to make sure I could get out. Speaking of which, I pulled specs and info from the security feeds I'd accessed, and tagged it to work on later.

I walked up the last ramp surrounded by a crowd of humans and augmented humans, and on into the station mall. There was no fringe travelers' area, with cheap transient hostels and vending kiosks. It went straight into multi-levels of expensive shops and offices, most in spheres, stacked into looming towers or hovering overhead. The feed was a maze of vids and ads and instructions and music, competing with the floating display surfaces and the holosculptures of giant waterfalls and trees and abstract art things. I'd seen similar, and better, on my shows, but seeing it in person was different. My camera angles weren't as good, for one thing. And the humans and augmented humans wandering around randomly were distracting from the view.

Oh, and there were downloads, sweet downloads, multiple entertainment feeds, way more than HaveRatton and Port FreeCommerce, hanging temptingly in the air. I picked a couple at random and started downloads. One of my queries had pulled up the station's actual index for residents, not the abbreviated one for tourists and transients, and I needed a place to stand still to review it. I headed toward one of the lower-level spheres.

It was a big shop, with lots of humans and augmented humans going in and out. I could do a shop. I'd done shops (one shop) before. No problem.

I tried to relax and look preoccupied as I took the ramp up to the entrance. The shop's feed ads said it sold advanced lifestyles. I don't know what that is and the explanations in the feed weren't helpful. Even some of the humans wandering around looked confused. I wandered with them into a central area where humans were watching a hovering display of products? Art and music inspired by products? It wasn't the enclosed booth I was hoping for, but it gave me a reason to stand still and stare while I reviewed my query results and the station index.

Not a surprise, I had turned up a dock listing for a shuttle with a company ID code, the only company code in the arrivals index. That was the shuttle the Preservation team had used to get here from the gunship.

It was . . . strange, knowing they were so close. Considering the size of the shuttle, they probably weren't staying on board. After a little delicate unraveling of the Port Authority's protected systems, I got a download of the docking contact index and matched the shuttle's entry with a physical address in a station hotel.

Three newssearch results popped up while I was deleting any trace of my intrusion from the PA's system, but they were old newsbursts from Port FreeCommerce. Just more useless speculation on where Mensah was and what she was doing, why she had disappeared.

None of my queries had turned up any mention of her.

I didn't have a lot of choice. The team from Preservation must be here to negotiate for Mensah's release, the only way they could proceed until Preservation scraped up enough currency to pay the company to violate TranRollinHyfa's docking ban. I needed intel before I could do anything, and they were my only potential source.

I left the shop, first making sure to do one loop of the aimless wander around the displays that the humans were doing.

I had to go meet some old friends.

Chapter Three

THE HOTEL WAS AT the far end of the station mall, in a quieter area with 60 percent less foot and drone traffic, next to a multi-level plaza. All the structures around it were office blocks or hotels, all were shaped like giant cones or cylinders, except for one either iconoclast or outdated sphere, which seemed to be holding on to its real estate despite the fact that the station had tried to block it from view with a large holo forest display.

I crossed one of the multi-level plazas, where humans and augmented humans were sitting singly and in groups at scattered tables and chairs, talking, viewing entertainment media on the displays, or working in their feeds. Surveillance was tight so I started one of the new codes I had written on the way here.

I had been thinking about other ways to look less like a SecUnit. (An obvious option was to pretend to eat or drink something, but that was tricky. I can do that if I have to, but only for a limited time. I don't have anything like a digestive system so I have to segregate a section of my lung to store it until I can expel it. Yes, it's just as awful as it sounds.) I'd decided on something more subtle and less disgusting. Humans, even augmented humans, subvocalize when they speak on the feed. I had written a quick set of code that I could run in background to mimic those jaw movements. (I pulled a selection of conversations from *Sanctuary Moon*, *Legends of the Fire*, and *Toward Tomorrow* to use as a template for the movements.) As I crossed the plaza toward the hotel I made sure my shoulders were relaxed and my expression was distracted. I picked up a camera feed from one of the drones watching the plaza for a look. Operating in concert with my code to mimic human breathing patterns and small random movements, it was perfect. Well, perfect for me. Let's say 98 percent perfect.

The Preservation group's hotel had a big terraced entrance with transparent walls and a wide doorway. A track for the station's pipe transport ran through a transparent upper floor of the structure, so you could see passengers disembarking and boarding inside when the chain of pipe capsules arrived. (I could see them via the higher-flying drones; the other humans in the plaza couldn't.)

I identified two potential hostiles sitting at tables in the plaza.

At the hotel entrance, I blended with a crowd of humans and augmented humans who were watching a floating advertising display that was showing funny short videos.

(Some were pretty good so I saved them to permanent storage.) It also gave me a place to stand while I worked my way into the hotel's security system. I had the improved version of my RaviHyral code routine to remove myself from camera views ready to deploy if needed.

When the video display started to repeat, I followed another group of humans through the entrance. I probably sound confident, but the scan at the arched doorway made my human skin prickle. I knew the kind of chance I was taking in coming here.

The lobby was a series of wide platforms with seating. It also had giant hanging biospheres full of simulated planetary skies, all displaying different weather. Ostensibly they were there to obscure the view of the seating platforms and provide some privacy, but they actually had the security system's cameras and scanners along the rims. As I watched myself through the cameras I spotted four more potential hostiles, all augmented humans. One was clearly in the feed, reviewing the scan results, and the others were moving around, doing visual sweeps.

No telling if they were GrayCris or Palisade, though if they were the hotel would know they were here. I couldn't tell if they were looking for me; there were no standing alerts in the security comm feed. Though from their affect they were paying close attention to augmented humans wearing any kind of hood, hat, or scarf, or face-obscuring tattoos, cosmetics, or ornaments. Me, a generic type augmented human person with my hood folded down on my back, didn't get a second glance.

This is why humans shouldn't do their own security.

I went up the ramp to the check-in platform, followed the directional feed with its welcoming musical theme and instructions to a kiosk, and booked a room with one of Gerth's hard currency cards.

Yes, I did enjoy doing that.

I took the rear exit off the platform to the pod junction and followed five humans into the first pod to arrive. It was a limited system, no outside connections, and would only take you to the room section now tied to your ID marker by the hotel's feed, or the lobbies and public entertainment sections. The pod took us to our sections in order of arrival, so it gave me a chance to watch the system in operation and copy its code. It took me to my section and I followed the feed map to my room.

It opened at the authorization the hotel had attached to my ID marker and at that brilliant moment I discovered there were no interior camera views or audio surveillance. Stupid hotel. I had probably even paid extra for it.

Still, the room was bigger and much nicer than the cabins I'd had on the passenger transports. I did a quick walk-through to scan for anomalies, then dropped my bag and lay down on the bed. (It was huge. Why have a bed that could easily accommodate four medium to large humans when you only had one hook for towels in the bath facility? Were the humans supposed to share the towel?) The wall across from the unnecessarily large bed was all display surface. To keep me company, I sent an episode of *Rise and Fall of Sanctuary Moon* to it to play—holy shit, the humans were almost actual size in the long shots—and then I got to work.

So there were no camera feeds from the rooms, but the cameras in the corridors were picking up humans and augmented humans as they moved through the connecting passages and used the transport pods to go to and from the lobbies and the three sections of food and club areas. (Whatever "clubs" were. The things going on there didn't seem to match my lexicon definition.) There was also a transport link to the pipe train level.

I worked my way carefully into the system, alert for traps. Without room cameras I was going to have to do this the hard way.

Like most surveillance systems on non-secure installations, this one didn't save their recordings permanently and supposedly deleted their archives after a waiting period. Note I said "supposedly." Of course, the hotel was datamining.

The mining was only on the conversations in the public areas and corridors, but then that was what I needed. I found the stored archives from the past twenty cycles, took over one of the routines that was processing it (it was separating out the boring bits from the juicy business conversations that would need to be sent to a human or bot monitor for review), and redirected it to search for my keyword set.

Eight minutes and thirty-seven seconds later, my captured routine turned up a sizable set of hits. I got the timestamps, then released the routine back to its job of searching for proprietary financial information. The timestamps let me know which archives to check for the camera surveillance.

I made some room in my temp storage, downloaded the first archive, and started my scans. I was reviewing it all myself instead of using a quicker and more efficient facial recognition scan on the collected data. That type of scan is only 62 percent reliable under most conditions and while that's fine for half-assed company security work, I didn't want to miss my targets. It turned out I could have started there instead of wasting the eight minutes, because in the first pass I caught an image of Ratthi in a corridor, walking toward a pod junction, timestamp sixteen hours and twenty-seven minutes minus present time.

Gotcha.

I kept reviewing the surveillance. Ratthi should have

put in some time reviewing it, too, or at least looking around a little, because two potential hostiles followed him to the junction. They didn't try to get on the same pod, but they clearly had access to the security system, because they were there when I picked Ratthi up in the lobby again. They followed him to the stores and vending areas in the hotel's lower level, then back to his room. Now that I knew to focus on that section of the hotel, I was able to eliminate a lot of video from other camera feeds, and within three minutes I picked up both Gurathin and Pin-Lee. All three were being followed, whenever they went out.

This wasn't unexpected, given that GrayCris had to know they were here. But I'd been doing some risk assessments in background and there was a scenario where this was a trap for me, where the Preservation team was bait.

Mensah might be the face of the group of political entities and companies determined to get GrayCris for killing their citizens/employees. But I was the one who had made the recordings of the most important evidence, I was the active component of the company SecSystem who had collected and stored all that data. If I was shown to be unreliable, compromised, whatever, then the SecSystem's data could be called into question and that might help GrayCris' case.

Another possibility was that the Preservation team

had been contacted by GrayCris and asked to lure me here in exchange for Mensah's release. Yeah, that possibility was no fun at all.

I watched Ratthi on the recordings, but the automated system had had no reason to zoom in and the resolution wasn't good enough for a real evaluation. But I ran a few of my archived records from the survey mission: Ratthi walking when he was tired after a long day, absorbed in a conversation as he walked with Arada and Overse, laughing and pretending to defend himself as Pin-Lee threw a cushion at him, running as we frantically loaded a hopper to escape.

I wanted to say he walked through this hotel like it was a prison, but I wasn't sure. Real humans don't act like the ones in the media.

I'd just have to wait and see. (And yes, that was painfully stressful.)

The surveillance was an interesting problem, but not unsolvable. Everywhere but in the lobby, the hotel had its own secured feed, which it charged extra to access. To encourage use, the hotel was choking the public feed. This meant the security system already had code in place to redirect feed accesses. That was convenient for me. I set some alerts on the various feeds in play and started picking which shows I wanted to watch on my gigantic display surface. I only picked old favorites I had watched before, though, because I really needed to buckle down and work on some new code. With luck, I wouldn't need it, but... Let's face it, I would probably need it.

Five hours and seventeen minutes later Pin-Lee, Ratthi, and Gurathin left their room and headed toward the pod junction. Twenty-three seconds after they left their room, the system registered a door opening and closing in the same section. Two hostiles exited the room to follow the Preservation team, and I was able to set a redirect on the feed stream they were using to get orders and deliver reports.

I waited to see if the Preservation team were just going to one of the food service or entertainment areas. It would be safer (for everybody, but especially me) to approach them outside the hotel.

I checked the feed stream the two hostiles used to get their orders and saw my redirect had worked. They stopped at the pod junction, confused, waiting for the go-ahead from their controller. My redirect had sent that go-ahead to the housekeeping bots in another section. The redirect was set to expire and delete itself in two minutes and would look like a glitch due to the hotel's feed-choking.

The Preservation team took the pod to the lobby and

headed out through the front entrance. I reluctantly shut down my giant display surface and rolled off the bed.

Time to go to work.

I took my bag with me because it was likely I wouldn't come back here. (Yes, I was going to miss that display surface.) It also had my projectile weapon, and you never could tell when you might need armor-piercing fire power. (And I could hook my right hand on the strap, which gave me something to do with that arm. How humans decide what to do with their arms on a second-by-second basis, I still have no idea.)

I caught up with Pin-Lee, Ratthi, and Gurathin in the plaza, with no sign of any hostiles trailing them. I wasn't sure the Preservation team knew GrayCris was surveilling them, though Ratthi's shoulders seemed a little stiff, not the way he usually walked. Then they started up the stairs to the second-level seating area and Gurathin glanced back in what he probably thought was a totally casual and not at all suspicious way. Yeah, they knew.

No, he didn't spot me. I was using the drone cams to keep track of them so I could take another route through the plaza, the one that led under the platforms through the gardens and vending areas.

Gurathin said something to Pin-Lee as they crossed the plaza and they sped up a little, heading for the shopping block on the far side. It was a good place to avoid visual surveillance from a tail and also gave me time to make minor adjustments to the security cams so it was more difficult to track them. GrayCris security would realize by now that they had lost them and I wanted to make sure they couldn't pick them up again. I didn't know if GrayCris had paid off the station to get access to their public space security video, but it was better to be safe than sorry.

Pin-Lee led the other two on a convoluted route through the shopping block, through various stores and plazas, and ended up in an open garden seating area at the foot of another cone-shaped hotel. It was a good effort, designed to take them through six different private security jurisdictions and private feed areas, a good way to lose a tail trying to follow you using drones or security cams. It didn't lose me, of course, but it was a great way to lose normal (human) surveillance. And the seating area was surrounded by curtains of falling water, obscuring the view from the surrounding plazas and walkways.

I stopped outside the entrance, joining a small crowd of humans beside a store projecting more artsy product videos into the feed. On the hotel's security cam I watched

Pin-Lee and Gurathin have a short argument, which Ratthi tried to mediate, that ended with Gurathin and Ratthi taking a seat at a table and Pin-Lee walking away into the mercantile area next to the hotel's lobby.

I know, I could have contacted them by now, either by establishing a secure connection on their feeds, or just walking up and saying hi. I just . . . wasn't sure.

Okay, I was scared. Or nervous. Nervous-scared.

Were they my sort-of human friends? My clients? My ex-owners, though legally that was only Dr. Mensah. Were they going to see me and yell for help, alert security?

And if it was this hard with Ratthi and Pin-Lee (Gurathin had never liked me and it was mutual), what was it going to be like with Mensah, if I managed to get that far?

I didn't know if I could trust them. I wanted to. But I want a lot of things—freedom, unlimited downloads, new episodes of *Drama Sun Islands*—most of which I wasn't going to get.

I walked through the garden seating area, which was only 37 percent occupied, but Ratthi and Gurathin didn't notice me. I scanned them as I went by, and picked up Gurathin's augments but no energy signatures indicating weapons. Ratthi rubbed his eyes and sighed. Gurathin's hard mouth was actually betraying some dismay.

I went through the open doorway into the mercantile area, which was light on the usual vending machines but had a lot of kiosks for various businesses, including passenger transport lines, station real estate, planetary real estate in this system and others, a lot of banks, and security companies. (Not Palisade, which catered only to corporate clients.) The area security was robust, but I couldn't pick up any facial recognition scans. The feed was choked and privatized, any humans or augmented humans not registered with the hotel required to pay a fee to use it, and the security was all focused on theft-prevention. At the far end of the space was an access to a transit platform; it didn't lead to the pipe, but to something called "transit bubbles."

I found Pin-Lee standing at a kiosk for a local security company, her expression grim, but she hadn't put her hand in the access field yet. I saw tension in her body language, particularly in the way she held her head. Whatever it was she had come here to do, she didn't want to do it.

It hit me then, how all those cycles of watching Pin-Lee on our contract had made me trust her judgment. If she didn't want to do it, she probably had a good reason. I had to talk to her, give her another option.

If it had been one of the others, I would have figured out a different approach. For Pin-Lee, I just said, "Hi."

She barely glanced at me, her expression set with disinterest. Then she took another look, frowned, started to speak, then stopped herself. She still wasn't sure. I said, "We met on Port FreeCommerce." I couldn't resist adding, "I was the one in the transport box."

Her eyes widened, then narrowed. She forced her tense shoulders to relax, and she didn't make the mistake of looking around. She planted a smile on her face and said through gritted teeth, "What—How—"

"I came to find our friend," I said. "Do you want to get in a transit bubble?" Local mass transport is usually easy to secure against potential surveillance and security screens. (Yes, it's supposed to be the opposite. Yes, you should worry.)

She hesitated, then forced her smile wider. It looked fake and angry, but it was the thought that counted. "Sure."

We crossed the room and walked up the access ramp to the station. A burst of feed advertising explained that the bubbles were a cup-shaped lift platform lined with padded benches, with a transparent bubble shield over the top so the humans couldn't manage to fall out no matter how hard they tried. (The ad didn't describe it that way.) The bubbles floated along a set path over the commercial segments and were much slower than the transit pipes, so they were mostly used for sightseeing. They also looked convenient for awkward conversations.

Only a few humans were in the station, stepping out of a just-arrived bubble. We walked up to the first rack and I paid with another hard currency card and—Wow, that was three times the price of my last transient hostel. It's a good thing I don't have to eat.

Pin-Lee climbed in first, eyeing me with what I wanted to interpret as discreet wariness but maybe wasn't. I sat down on the opposite bench and selected the option for an overhead tour of this segment's shopping park. The door sealed and the bubble floated up to join the line of others passing over the hotel.

The bubble had a camera feed, but it was the kind meant to alert on certain words, sounds, and motions, probably only there to cut down on random murders. I blocked its audio feed and said, "Clear."

She glared at me. "You left."

Somehow I hadn't expected that. I said, "Mensah said I could learn to do anything I wanted. I learned to leave."

"You could have told her what you wanted. We—she—we were worried, okay." My gaze was on the view behind her, using the bubble's camera to study her face. She pressed her lips together, cutting off whatever she was going to say next. Then she regrouped and continued, "I saw the goodbye message you sent her. It's not like she didn't realize that we'd fucked up the whole situation."

I was having an emotion, and I hate that. I'd rather have nice safe emotions about shows on the entertainment media; having them about things real-life humans said and did just led to stupid decisions like coming to TranRollinHyfa. And they hadn't fucked up the whole situation. Parts of it, sure. But it's not like I knew what to do with me, either. "I don't want to talk about it."

She sighed, a tired but angry sigh, and pressed her fingers to her forehead. I had to quell an impulse to tap my nonexistent MedSystem and ask for a diagnosis. She said, "So where the fuck did you go? And what are you doing here?" She hesitated warily. "Are you working for someone, on contract?"

That was the whole point of leaving. "Either I'm Mensah's property, and I work for her, or I'm a free agent and I work for myself."

Glare intensifying. "Okay, so what did you hire yourself to do?"

That was an interesting way to put it. I kind of liked it. And it felt so weird to be talking to a human like this, a human who knew what I was. I didn't have to force myself to stare at Pin-Lee's face, worry that my expressions were normal. Abene had known I was a SecUnit, but she hadn't known I was me. "I've been traveling, and I saw a newsburst that said Mensah was missing. Did they trick her into coming here, or was she abducted?"

Her eyes narrowed again, but this time more in speculation. "You've really just been wandering around watching that serial. We were afraid GrayCris might catch you, but they kept demanding you be submitted as part of the evidence process. It seemed like they would have let us know if they had you, gloated about it."

"I've been wandering around watching a lot of serials." I waited. Pin-Lee had always been the tough one, and it took her time to let down her guard. Like all the others, I had hundreds of hours of stored audio and video of her. I didn't need to review it to know her nerves were stretched thin from fear for Mensah, from the responsibility for the others' lives.

She said finally, "So you came to help us. Why should I trust you? You obviously don't trust us."

If I could answer that, I'd probably be a lot better off. I didn't trust them, not with some things. I had no idea why they should trust me. "I pulled a status report from the company gunship. They aren't going to help you unless the station lifts the docking prohibition. You're on your own. Or you're on your own with Ratthi and Gurathin, which may be worse."

She grimaced. "I forgot what an asshole you are."

Well, yeah. I said, "I need intel to make a plan."

She looked at the view, and winced a little at the flashing ad display circling the spire we were passing. "They took her off Port FreeCommerce, after a meeting with DeltFall representatives. Some of the families of the victims had traveled in to personally collect the remains, there were a lot of people there, it was emotional. She stepped away for a minute afterward, and she was gone. The security cams showed the moment when they grabbed her, but by that time they had already taken her off the station. With some help from our diplomatic corps on Preservation, I convinced the company that this was their problem, that they had fucked up so badly with our survey bond that they owed us. Then GrayCris sent a demand that Preservation drop our suit against them and make a public announcement to that effect. We've done that, and now we're here to negotiate a ransom." Her expression tightened. "We've got people on Preservation working to free up assets, but right now we don't have nearly as much as they want."

So I was right, and GrayCris did need money. "But no company contract support?"

"Not after TRH refused to let them dock. They did give us a key for the fail-safe interface implant Mensah bought in case of emergency, but Gurathin said it's blocked because she's being held somewhere in the torus above us, behind the main station security barrier, and it's dampening the signal."

"Do you have it with you?" I asked. It might be blocked for Gurathin, but not for me.

She unsealed an inside pocket on her jacket and handed me the key, which was designed to look like a feed-accessible memory clip. I downloaded the address information and spent one minute and forty-three seconds trying to access Mensah's implant. So it was actually blocked for me, too. "Gurathin may be right about the main station security barrier." I hated to say it.

Pin-Lee slumped in disappointment. "We don't have much longer to raise the ransom. I was going to try to hire a local security company to help us, and just hope the one I picked hadn't been paid off by GrayCris." She looked away from the window, eyeing me again. "Speaking of pay-offs, the company is playing a double game, right?"

I was glad Pin-Lee had thought of that already and wasn't going to deny reality. "There's a ninety-five percent chance," I told her. The company is like an evil vending machine, you put money in and it does what you want, unless somebody else puts more money in and tells it to stop. GrayCris' best option at this point was to pour as much money in as possible.

Pin-Lee groaned and rubbed her face. "I'm almost glad you're here."

Chapter Four

WHEN OUR BUBBLE RETURNED to the station, I went to a hotel kiosk to book a room and Pin-Lee went to get the others. She thought we needed to talk as a group in private. I sort of did, too. (We could have done it via the feed in the garden seating area, but I didn't trust the humans not to wave their arms and draw attention.)

I took a pod up to the room and of course there was no security feed inside because of the stupid hotel wanting to lure humans in with promises of room privacy so it could record them in the public spaces. This hotel was less expensive than the previous one but the pretty quotient was about the same. And the feed was choked, unless of course you happened to know how to get around that.

The room was a lot more practical, with a normal-sized bed folded up into the wall to leave extra space for chairs, and a display surface that only took up a fourth of a wall instead of all of it, and a bathing facility with more room for towels. SecUnits are never allowed to sit down or use human furniture whether on or off duty, so I sat in one of the chairs and put my feet up on the table. Then I took my feet off the table because it wasn't comfortable. I entertained myself by infiltrating the hotel's security system while I waited.

When the room's feed signaled that they were at the door, I told it to open. I was in my best casual pose, and *Sanctuary Moon* was on the display surface. (I was actually redirecting the audio as chaff for a suspicious monitor that the hotel might be using to record inside the rooms, even though the booking agreement certified complete in-room privacy.)

Pin-Lee elbowed the other two in and let the door slide closed. She had clearly told them already, because Ratthi was grinning. He said, "You look great! What have you been doing?"

Gurathin's expression I interpreted as appalled. I still don't like you, either.

"Ratthi, later," Pin-Lee said. She stepped past them and dropped down into the other armchair. "SecUnit doesn't need to tell us where it's been or what it's been doing unless it wants to. We need to focus on how to free Mensah."

I didn't expect that and I was glad I was looking at the display surface. The lack of a camera was going to make this awkward, at least for me. I could sort of see everyone in the decorative reflective material at the top of the walls, but that was inadequate.

Gurathin took a breath to say something and Pin-Lee pointed at him. "If you're going to argue—"

Gurathin grimaced and held up his hands in surrender. "No, no argument. I just don't see how SecUnit is going to help. They won't release Mensah without the ransom, and we don't have it."

Ratthi told me, "Our company liaison said they were probably holding her in the GrayCris corporate headquarters in the upper torus, past the main station security barrier, where visitors aren't allowed. Now that you're here—can we just get her out, and escape?"

It was a dumb idea, so I needed to quash it immediately. I'd already secured a private feed connection between the four of us and now I sent my annotated station map into it. "The problem isn't that GrayCris' corporate headquarters is in the upper torus." I sent the image to the room's display surface, then had it zoom out and plot the route between here and there. I had all the security checkpoints light up, annotating the ones that barred entrance to anyone with a non-station citizen ID, which was all of them. "It's that we would be leaving territory controlled by neutral TRH security and entering GrayCris' corporate jurisdiction." I didn't know what they'd do to me, now that my data port was nonfunctional and they couldn't take control of me. There was a long list of alternatives, including just shooting me until I ceased to function and various other things that would seem sensible and practical to them and like torture to me. Whatever, it wasn't a good idea to get caught, basically. "In this lower ring, GrayCris has to negotiate with and pay off TRH, and any private security service or entity who has jurisdiction, for each operation, which gives us a slight advantage."

"Oh." Ratthi sat back in his chair, dismayed. "Even with support from the bond company gunship? I mean, the company said they won't violate the TRH edict to come aboard the station, but they are out there, with big guns..."

Frankly I hoped they stayed out there. I said, "If GrayCris can't make you disappear, they want to delay you. They're probably raising the money to buy off the company. The gunship is also here to exert pressure on GrayCris while the company is negotiating with their reps back on Port FreeCommerce. That ransom GrayCris asked for Mensah's return will probably go straight to the company, as part of the pay-off."

Ratthi was clearly shocked. Pin-Lee let out a frustrated breath and said, "That's what our diplomatic corps on Preservation thought."

Ratthi turned to her. "You didn't tell us that!"

Gurathin folded his arms. "I knew it."

I couldn't let that one go. I turned and gave him my best skeptical stare. Surprisingly, it worked. He admitted, "I suspected it."

Pin-Lee was asking Ratthi, "Did you want to know? I was hoping to get Mensah and get out of here before GrayCris managed to negotiate the payoff."

Ratthi groaned. "No, I didn't want to know. What happens to Mensah and us if GrayCris makes a deal with the company while we're here?"

Pin-Lee lifted a hand helplessly and Gurathin looked more sour. He said, "Guess."

I said, "It's possible GrayCris can't afford the payoff." They might be desperately trying to sell off their alien remnant and strange synthetic collection before even more word got out about Milu. It was against the corporate/political entity interdicts to have alien materials, which meant GrayCris could only trade in it as long as no one knew. The bond company wouldn't take alien remnants in payment unless they couldn't be traced to it. There was no chance of that now. Which meant GrayCris was that much more desperate.

In the reflection I watched Pin-Lee look at me. "Is there any way we—you—can get her out without the ransom?"

I had been running possible scenarios, partly to drown out the sound of humans making stupid suggestions.

(Not that I don't like that sound; it's sort of comforting and familiar, in an annoying way.) "It would be tricky," I said. By tricky I meant I was getting an average of an 85 percent chance of failure and death, and it was only that low because my last diagnostic said my risk assessment module was wonky. (I know, that explains a lot about me.) "We need to find a way to make them bring her outside the main station security barrier so that I can track her location via her company implant."

I was going to suggest a hack of their messaging systems, not that I had any idea how to get into those systems yet. Or if that would even work, since presumably a high-security prisoner transfer would need to be signed off by a human or augmented human supervisor who might ask unanswerable questions. But Pin-Lee turned to Ratthi and Gurathin and said, "We could offer them the ransom and arrange an exchange in one of these hotels."

Ratthi nodded slowly, considering it. "But how much do they know about our finances? Will they know it's a lie?"

Pin-Lee made an abrupt gesture. "We don't have to show them a hard currency card."

Gurathin leaned forward. "I can come up with a convincing feed document listing some of Preservation's off-planet assets. They don't need to know that those assets can't be exchanged yet. But once we get them to bring her to the meeting—"

It wasn't a terrible plan. It probably wasn't even in the top ten of terrible plans. I said, "We don't have to get them to bring her all the way to the meeting. We just need to get them to move her outside that security barrier so I can find her."

Gurathin turned to me. "If they do, you can take her away from them, no matter how many guards?"

I was beginning to think Gurathin's asshole expression was some congenital condition he had no control over. I said, "The more guards the better."

He lifted his brows. "Are you going to kill them?"

Scratch that, Gurathin's asshole expression is due to him being an asshole.

I could lie, I could say oh no, I won't kill them, I'm a nice SecUnit. I think I was going to say that, or the more believable version of it. Instead what came out was, "If I have to."

There was a little silence. Pin-Lee had her lips folded in and didn't say anything. But I recognized her committed expression from my archived video, from the moment in the hopper when the satellite connection dropped, and she voted to keep going to DeltFall. Ratthi's face was a study in conflicted resolution. Gurathin just said, "You feel you're qualified to make that call."

I said, "I'm the security expert. You're the humans who walk in the wrong place and get attacked by angry fauna. I have extracted living clients from situations that were less than nine percent survivable. I'm more than qualified to make that call."

Gurathin sat back, slowly. I stood up. "I'm going to wait in the lobby. Contact me when you make your decision."

Pin-Lee held up a hand. "Wait, we've made our decision." She looked at Ratthi. "Right?"

He set his jaw. "Right. This is GrayCris we're talking about. They mean to kill Mensah and us, too, if they can."

Gurathin said, "We're agreed."

I was already standing up. I said, "I'm going to the lobby anyway," and left.

I wasn't sulking or hiding. The lobby was a better strategic position.

This lobby was on multiple levels and had large square biozones depicting different ecologies, with furniture arranged around them. It looked nice, inviting humans to sit around and discuss proprietary information in the hotel's choked feed so the hotel could record it and sell it to the highest bidder. I also had inputs monitoring the upper-level plaza entrance and the transit lobby.

I found a place to sit where a biozone showing a storm on a gas giant blocked me from the view of the other seating areas.

On the feed the humans settled some details of what I was designating as Operation Not Actually A Completely Terrible Plan.

I sent Pin-Lee a note saying they should arrange to meet the contact here, as their hotel already had GrayCris crawling all over it and so far this one was clear. Pin-Lee forwarded it to the others and they agreed. They didn't even have anything to collect from their old room. (They were traveling light, with only a few hygiene items, Pin-Lee's medication, Gurathin's specialized tool kit, and Ratthi's lucky spare interface, all of which Gurathin was carrying in a shoulder bag.)

(I thought how odd it was, that I didn't have to worry about human stuff anymore. It felt like I'd been carrying/stepping over/climbing around human stuff in human habitations for my entire existence. Probably because I had.)

Again, it wasn't a bad plan given our circumstances. Timing was going to be tight. I didn't know the route GrayCris would use to bring Mensah to the meeting point. I would have to wait until they moved into range of the hotel's security cams. Which was fine, except it didn't leave us much time for our exit strategy, such as it was.

Then Pin-Lee said, "Are we ready?" The other two agreed. Then she called up the hotel's in-room comm access on the display surface and made the call to their GrayCris contact.

With the comm active, I got a visual from the display surface even though I didn't have a cam view in the room. Not that there was much to see: the GrayCris contact had the visual blanked on their end. Pin-Lee stated that she had the ransom and where she wanted Mensah brought for the exchange. GrayCris said they wanted the ransom now and would then release Mensah, blah, blah, blah, but it sounded perfunctory to me, compared to other hostage exchanges I'd witnessed. GrayCris really wanted this payoff. Pin-Lee argued for two minutes with them before they gave in, though they wanted to send a representative in first to look at the funds authorization.

After Pin-Lee closed the comm, Ratthi said, "Oh, I hope we're doing this right."

Gurathin said, grimly (the way he said everything, basically), "We'll find out soon enough."

Pin-Lee said, "It'll be all right." (Mensah would have made it sound reassuring; Pin-Lee obviously meant it to sound reassuring and it came out like she wanted them to just shut up.)

Gurathin came down to the lobby to wait for the GrayCris representative and took a seat in plain view on a lower platform, so stiff he looked more like a SecUnit than I did.

Well, in his defense it was a nerve-racking situation. I couldn't risk the distraction of watching media, but I checked my storage space, and noted that I still had a comfortingly high number of episodes left in the new show I was watching. It helped, a little.

One reason I was nervous was because if this went well and I wasn't shot to pieces, I would be seeing Mensah again.

On the way to RaviHyral, ART had said that PreservationAux was my crew. I don't know if ART was being naive or it thought I was. Okay, maybe I was naive enough at the time to think it might be a little true. Then after RaviHyral, I had given up on the idea. Then I had somehow decided I would get evidence for Mensah from Milu and I had seen Don Abene when Miki . . . died and for a while I was back to the "maybe it was a little true" point again.

But sitting here in a hotel lobby, watching a biozone and running every not-a-SecUnit behavioral code I had, the fantasy fell apart. The hard reality was that I didn't know what Mensah was to me.

Even after Miki, I still didn't want to be a pet robot.

Up in the room, Pin-Lee was pacing slowly and trying not to grind her teeth and Ratthi had gone to the bathroom three times. Gurathin was just sitting and staring. Then he said over the feed, *Are you there, SecUnit?*

No, I left, I said, *I've decided to live here and just move from hotel to hotel, watching the entertainment feed.*

Okay, so that did sound like a much better idea than I meant it to.

There was a pause, then he said, *I'm not your enemy. I'm just cautious.*

I don't care about your opinion, I said, and then immediately wished I'd put myself on a one-second delay so I could delete it. It made it sound like I did care. Which I didn't.

One minute crawled by. Then two. Gurathin said, *What did you do, while you were gone? Where did you go?*

I didn't want to answer, because I didn't want to talk about it, but it seemed weirdly petty to just ignore him. I pulled a selection of video from the trip with Ayres and the others on the way to HaveRatton, mostly exchanges I'd tagged so I could critique my performance later. (A few times I'd broken up fights, been forced to give relationship advice, and the infamous Cracker Wrapper in the Sink Incident.) I cut it together, labeled it "Murderbot Impersonates an Augmented Human Security Consultant," and sent it to Gurathin.

He was still watching it when the GrayCris representative walked into the lobby from the main entrance.

There was nothing physical to set him apart from the

other humans and augmented humans wandering in and out. He was a tall pale human, with long light-colored hair, and he was wearing one of the many local variations of business attire: a dark long-sleeved jacket that went to the knees, over wide pants.

I tapped Gurathin and he stopped the video play.

The GrayCris rep paused and a flash of annoyance crossed his face. He'd encountered the choked hotel feed. The hotel system registered the charge to a station credit account and then gave him access. I caught the results of the routine scan from the hotel's security drone: no weapons, just interface activity. A brief analysis of the drone's read gave me a 65 percent probability that he had something on him to falsify the scan. So he was probably armed and probably carrying a secured comm device.

I had access to his feed but I didn't figure it would do much good. If he had a device on him to fake readings for a security scan, then he had to know a choked hotel feed was hardly the best place for operational communication.

It was the hypothetical secured comm device I had to worry about. Whatever it was, it would need to use the hotel's relay to reach the station's comm network.

The GrayCris rep did a visual scan of the lobby and

obviously recognized Gurathin, probably from intel obtained by GrayCris on Port FreeCommerce. He went toward Gurathin, who stood to meet him. He said, "Gurathin? I'm Serrat, here at the request of Pin-Lee." He was calm, confident, with a hint of a friendly smile.

Gurathin's asshole effect must come in handy at times like this. With a deeply unimpressed expression, he said, "This way," and started toward the pod junction.

I tapped Pin-Lee and Ratthi to warn them, and continued a visual sweep for hostiles. Like those two humans, strolling casually through the main entrance, casually pausing to casually look around, then casually proceeding to the stairs that led to the lounge/food service area. (Right, so they really weren't that bad, but I'd been sitting here long enough to analyze the traffic patterns. Humans who walk in looking for something, or are genuinely confused about where to go next, tended to move in erratic ways, their attention caught by the biozones, the feed indicators for the ramp that takes you to the registration area, etc. Compared to that, the hostiles were easy to spot.)

Maybe too easy? The hotel drone scan came back negative, but with that same suspicious pattern as the GrayCris rep. (It was suspicious to me; I've fooled a lot of drone scans.)

I marked two more potential hostiles exiting a pipe capsule in the transit lobby, and a check-in with my friends the plaza drone cams showed more outside the hotel's plaza entrance.

Yeah, I had a bad feeling about that, too. But I was still monitoring the security system, and there were no alerts, no anomalous signals.

I meant to stay here until the exchange was arranged, but now I got up and headed for the pod junction. I had one input riding Gurathin's feed. He and Serrat had just stepped out of the pod. Gurathin had made the whole trip awkwardly silent. I was reluctantly impressed.

I was in the pod and at the right section by the time Gurathin and Serrat reached the room. There was no cover in the corridor, so I told the pod to hold and notify hotelEnvironmentAccessAndMobilitySystem (MobSys for short) not to take action on any maintenance requests. (It sounds like a lot of trouble just to stop a pod, but if I didn't do it that way it would have crashed the system. Literally, if I interfered with MobSys' pod traffic control. And by literally, I mean pods full of humans and augmented humans crashing into each other.)

They were in the room now and Pin-Lee was saying, "We have the currency your corporation asked for. Some of it had to come from liquidated assets, and I've received notice that they're ready to transfer. I won't produce the list or send the authorization until we see Dr. Mensah."

Serrat answered, "I assure you, she's already on her way here, escorted by a security detail. I do need to see the transfer authorization."

I had one input monitoring Mensah's implant, but it wasn't pinging yet. I also had a couple of analyses going, estimating distances and potential routes between here and the upper torus, and I was working on a contingency for the port in case they had real security (i.e., SecUnits from Palisade or one of the other local bond companies) with them. It could potentially get disastrously complicated, but I still thought it was doable.

Then it got disastrously complicated.

In the feed, Ratthi said, *Uh, SecUnit? Please help.*

Like an idiot my first reaction was to try to switch to the helmet cam Ratthi wasn't wearing. I had no camera in the room, just audio, and all I could hear was breathing. (This was the flaw in Plan 1A. There had been no way to get a camera in the room in the time we had, or at least not one undetectable to the security screen the GrayCris rep would come prepared to make.) Then Pin-Lee said, "That won't get you the money. And money is what you need, right? What GrayCris needs right now to call off the bond company."

Serrat said flatly, "That is not a transfer authorization. That is just a list of assets. What are you playing at?"

Scrambling for my inputs, scrambling to make sure I had control of hotelSecSys, I caught the signal Serrat had just used his comm device to send. It had to be an emergency abort for the hostage release, and possibly a signal for his backup to come in shooting. With zero time for finesse, I killed the main hotel relay, then had to take down two secondary relays that tried to activate to pick up the traffic. Then I found Serrat's connection to the hotel feed and blocked it. I was busy, so my buffer said, *Dr. Ratthi, please describe the problem.*

Ratthi's feed voice was nervous. *He has a gun. It's small, um, palm-sized. Energy weapon, I think too small for projectiles.*

On audio, Gurathin said, "That's the transfer document we were given—"

"And that's a ridiculous lie," Serrat said.

Keep him talking, I sent to Pin-Lee. I didn't want him wondering why his backup hadn't sent an acknowledgment. I'd just discarded Plan Actually Not All That Terrible and shifted to Plan Approaching Terrible. I stepped out of the pod, and released it back to MobSys as I strode down the corridor. My scan picked up a moving target around the curve and I slowed down to a casual stroll that looked just as fake and awkward as the version performed by the GrayCris reps in the lobby. But my connection to hotelSecSys showed another room door had opened in this section twenty seconds ago and the chance that the approaching humans were hostiles was less than ten percent.

Two small humans rounded the curve of the corridor, very occupied with adjusting shoulder bags and head coverings. They passed me but it slowed my progress to target and I had to walk past the room door until they were out of sight, then wait for them to reach the junction and step into a pod. Then I moved.

I muted my feed audio, which was Pin-Lee, Ratthi, and Gurathin loudly objecting to the gun and protesting their innocence and that the funds transfer bank must have made a mistake and Ratthi was a biologist and he didn't understand all this esoteric financial stuff and etc. I pressed my ear to the door and upped my hearing, and managed to pick up Serrat saying, "I don't have time to teach you the facts of corporate relations."

That gave me his relative position. Then I hit the door release.

As the door slid open, Serrat started to turn toward me. I crossed the room, grabbed his wrist and forced it down, and sent a targeted pulse through my arm to fry the power cell of his tiny, cute little gun. Then I used my other forearm to pin his throat to the wall. This all happened really fast.

Serrat made a strangled noise and tried to shoot me. Even if the gun had still worked, it would have hit me in the shin, which would have just made me that much more pissed off. I squeezed his wrist and he dropped the gun. He was still holding the comm device.

Ratthi had fallen over a chair trying to get out of the way, and Pin-Lee lost a few seconds getting around him. Gurathin staggered but lunged forward and grabbed Serrat's other hand. He pried Serrat's fingers open and Pin-Lee plucked the comm device out.

"It's activated?" Ratthi asked, struggling to his feet.

I said, "I've blocked it and his feed." One of my inputs was the management channel on the hotel feed, which was already filling up with complaints about the comm failure. I had also taken out the connection between the hotel's choked feed and the station feed. (Which implies I did it intentionally, but I had been in a hurry and just slammed down everything with a signal.) (Yeah, so much for making this a stealth operation.)

Serrat breathed hard, and this close my scan picked up elevated pulse and sweat gland activity. He said, "So this is the supposedly missing SecUnit."

I checked hotelSecSys' view of the lobby and spotted the two GrayCris backups. They hadn't reacted yet, still pretending to be casual around the vending machines, but oh shit did I need to get the hotel feed's connections back up before they noticed.

Pin-Lee leaned down to grab the gun off the floor. "Is Mensah really being brought here? Was that a lie?"

No response from the implant yet, I told her on the feed. I could still access the station feed, and that's what would carry the implant's signal. If GrayCris was really bringing her here, they hadn't crossed the main station security barrier yet.

So the plan wasn't a clusterfuck, it was just circling the clusterfuck target zone, getting ready to come in for a landing.

Serrat said to Pin-Lee, "You're the liars, thinking you could fool us with that ridiculous fake document. Order this thing to let me go. You're violating station law, threatening me with a deadly weapon."

"What deadly weapon?" Ratthi demanded. He gestured to the gun in Pin-Lee's hand. "You threatened us with a deadly weapon, we could call station security on you!"

In the feed, Gurathin said, *We can't call station security.*
I know that! Ratthi sent back. *I'm bluffing.*

Pin-Lee said, "He means SecUnit. SecUnit is the deadly weapon." She hesitated, then sent to me in the feed, *I'm going to touch you, don't freak out.*

Uh, okay. I tapped back an acknowledgment because I was frantically working to bring the hotel's main and secondary relays back up and I had to get in ahead of the repair techs.

Pin-Lee put her hand on my shoulder and I did not freak out. She leaned in toward Serrat and said, "This is not a deadly weapon. This is a person. An angry person, who wants you to answer the question. Are you bringing Mensah here?"

He smiled at her. "I was. I've signaled our security officer to cancel the exchange. They know where I am, and they'll be here soon. Since you've violated station law by bringing in a privately owned SecUnit, no one will help you."

"You need the ransom to pay off the bond company, right?" Pin-Lee said. I hadn't looked away from Serrat, though most of my attention was on the admittedly rough job I was doing on the hotel relays and still listening for Mensah's implant. She added, "Surely GrayCris has assets it can sign over. Or is it revenge?"

Serrat's face slipped into a skeptical sneer. He didn't take them seriously, which, sure, I can see why. If you were GrayCris and regularly murdered humans as part of your job, the wrath of three research surveyors from a noncorporate backwater planet probably didn't fill you with fear. And he was certain they were controlling me somehow. He said, "Revenge? You buy a SecUnit and send it to Milu to expose an essential GrayCris asset operation. You and your little planetary polity have the audacity to think you can compete with a corporation—what did you expect to happen?"

Pin-Lee must have been taken aback, but she said, "GrayCris attacked us first. GrayCris started this. All we want is the return of Dr. Mensah."

In the feed, a baffled Ratthi said, *Milu?*

With his augment, Gurathin had some information storage. He said, *That was in a newsburst, they asked Mensah about it. It's an abandoned terraforming platform.*

I got the hotel's relays back up and the activity on the hotel's management feed began to drop immediately. The two GrayCris targets in the lobby still hadn't noticed anything wrong. Still nothing from the implant.

They weren't bringing her. This had all been for nothing. All of it, Milu, Miki's death, the trip here, everything. I said, "Milu was my idea. I'm a rogue unit."

He ignored me, but he said to Pin-Lee, "A rogue unit would have left a trail of dead bodies across this station."

I said, "Maybe I wanted the trail to start here."

He made eye contact with me, and his pupils widened slightly.

I added, "You people are so naive."

It was a really good thing that right then Mensah's

implant pinged. I hadn't completely decided to crush Serrat's windpipe, I was just entertaining the idea. Instead I pulled him away from the wall and choked him out.

From the humans it was all "Wait!" "No!" "Um—"

"I'm not going to kill him," I said, and dumped him on the couch. "I know what I'm fucking doing."

Pin-Lee had tuned her feed to the implant and now clawed the key out of her jacket to check it. "She's moving, she's—Can you tell—"

I was already matching the ping to my station maps. "They're on a transit pipe." I had to go, now. I told them, "You need to get back to your shuttle. Leave him; by the time he's conscious GrayCris will already know what we're doing. Don't take his comm or his gun with you, StationSec can scan for them. Go down to the hotel's first-level garden court and take the bubble transit to the next shopping complex, then take pipe transit from there."

I was out the door before they could do more than take in enough air to object. The corridor was clear so I sprinted to the pod junction. In the feed, I sent, *The GrayCris group with Mensah is less than two minutes out and counting, you need to be out of the hotel before they get here. She'll meet you at your shuttle. Do not try to contact me on the feed. If they buy off StationSec, they could trace us.*

We're going, we're going, Ratthi sent back, and hotelSecSys told me the room door had just opened and closed. *Be careful—*

I'm breaking contact, Ratthi, I told him, and stepped into the pod.

I shut my risk assessment module down.

Chapter Five

WHEN THE TRANSIT PIPE with GrayCrisSec and Dr. Mensah arrived, I was in a pod, paused and ready.

The hotelSecSys cams showed me the GrayCris group exiting the pipe onto the platform as waiting passengers scattered out of the way. The hostiles were in plain clothes but with visible weapons; this obviously wasn't a covert operation for them, so that meant StationSec as well as hotelSec had been paid for access.

And they had an armored SecUnit with them.

This was still doable. (My wonky Risk Assessment Module would probably have informed me that everything was great.) There was a pause while the group encountered the hotel's choked feed and got someone to authorize a payment. (I guess you could pay off the management to let you bring in a SecUnit and weapons and do a hostage exchange, but they drew the line at giving you free feed access.)

The hotel's transit station was three levels tall, with one open level above the platform where the pipe stopped and one below. The one above was currently running a holographic thunderstorm display, and the one below was cycling through overhead views of various art installations, or at least that's what the feed tag said it was doing.

I just had an idea, which I filed under save-for-later.

The hostiles took Mensah along the platform walkway toward the pod junction. She wasn't wearing any kind of restraints, but there were six of them plus the SecUnit. Two peeled off to take up positions in the transit station. That left four targets plus the SecUnit, the primary target.

SecUnits who haven't hacked their governor module like me can't hack feeds and systems like I can. Well, they could try, but their governor module would punish them and their Sec or HubSystem would report them and they would end up with a memory purge. (So if you decide to hack your governor module, you need to do a good job and get it right the first time.) The unit GrayCris had with them was your basic killing machine.

The SecUnit had a Palisade logo on its chest. The armor was a proprietary brand, a different configuration from company armor. No drones, though. (GrayCris should really have paid that extra bribe money to get the drones in.)

(Yes, I thought about hacking it. I had never hacked another SecUnit. I'd hacked a ComfortUnit, but it hadn't been trying to stop me. I couldn't afford the experiment.

If I tried and failed and it reported me, Mensah and the others would pay for it.)

They reached the junction and I delayed the pod's arrival to give me a little time. The SecUnit was scanning, checking for weapons on the humans in the transit station and for unauthorized comm and feed activity. I was too deep in the hotel feed for it to find me. (If I hadn't been able to hide my feed activity from other SecUnits, I would have been spare parts a long time ago.)

I made the connection to Mensah's implant and pinged her feed to test the security. None of the targets including primary reacted. Then I sent, *Hi, Dr. Mensah. It's me.* Her chest moved with a sharp breath and her head made a slight aborted motion. She had just conquered the urge to look around. One target glanced at her but the others didn't react. I added, *Try to answer me without subvocalizing.*

She didn't respond for 3.2 seconds and I had that long to wonder if she didn't want to talk to me. That would make this rescue 100 percent more awkward.

Then she said, *Prove you're you. Tell me your name.*

Okay, not that awkward. That was a relief. It also told me how bad her situation was, if she was worried about someone trying to trick her by posturing in her feed. I said, *It's Murderbot, Dr. Mensah.*

That conversation had been permanently deleted, so no one knew about it except the PreservationAux team. Assuming they hadn't told anyone else about it. Mensah obviously assumed it.

She responded immediately, *What are you doing here? You weren't captured?*

They must have told her that, because there was nothing like that in the newsfeeds. Disinformation, which is the same as lying but for some reason has a different name, is the top tactic in corporate negotiation/warfare. (There had been a whole episode about it on *Sanctuary Moon*.) I told her, *I came to help you, to get you to the port where Pin-Lee, Ratthi, and Gurathin are waiting with a company shuttle. It's dangerous, but less dangerous than staying where you are. Do I have a go to proceed?* I know, but somehow it was easier being formal about it.

She answered immediately, *Yes.*

I tapped her feed to acknowledge and backburnered it so I could concentrate on my ongoing relationship with hotelSecSys and my new best friend, MobSys. I checked the schematic I had pulled earlier. My operation had to take place in this section, at one of the junctions, because once the pod moved into the hotel's main network, it would be going too fast. Even if I could pull its direction info, I couldn't get ahead of it.

Splitting my attention between all the security camera

feeds I was monitoring was tricky, but not much trickier than listening to HubSystem, SecSystem, various client feeds, and vocal commands from confused and impatient humans while watching entertainment media. At least that's what I was telling myself. I'm not sure I could have done it before all the work on Milu had increased my processing space.

If I screwed this up ... I couldn't screw this up.

I selected what the MobSys told me was the most common destination, the hotel's club section. My pod started to move and two seconds into the trip, I asked MobSys for an emergency halt and hold in a low-traffic junction, but not to trigger any alarms for bot or human supervisors.

The pod stuttered to a halt. Part of the emergency protocol is to redirect any pods headed toward the site of the emergency call. Through MobSys, I felt pods all over the structure swooshing safely away through alternate passages.

I stepped out of my pod into the junction. It was an empty platform with two corridors curving away. I made sure the security camera would hold the image of an empty platform for the next six minutes. Then I got my projectile weapon out of my bag, loaded it, and held it down and to my side, angled back.

On the walkway camera feed, I saw the targets and Mensah get into their pod. I asked MobSys to please bring that pod here to the junction to assist with the emergency. As it arrived, I stepped into the waiting area and hit Dr. Mensah's feed again. *Dr. Mensah, at my signal, please drop to the floor of the pod in a crouch and cover your head.*

The doors slid open. Pod trips are so fast, I was figuring the humans would have a couple of seconds of confusion thinking they had reached their destination. I used those two seconds to snap their connection to the hotel feed, then I stepped forward like a normal dumb human wanting to get in the pod, careful to be at an angle where the SecUnit wouldn't see me. (The human operatives had helped by making it stand to the left side of the pod, instead of in the front where it should have been.)

A human target pushed forward. (In a completely unnecessary aggressive way; this is why humans suck at security so much even other humans don't want them to do it.) He snapped, "Back up, this is a corporate securi—"

I tapped Mensah's feed and she dropped. I already had the tough-with-apparently-unarmed-citizen target by the arm. I fired the energy weapon in my arm into his shoulder, pulled him toward me as he slumped, then lifted him up to shield my body.

Primary Target (the other SecUnit) was already in motion and shoved two human targets aside and brought its projectile weapon up. It couldn't fire because of my human shield and that bought me the extra second to fire three armor-piercing projectiles point-blank into the neck joint of its armor, then down into its knee joints.

(The neck joint was the kill shot, the knee joints were to make it drop, otherwise the armor might have made it freeze in place.)

I dropped my projectile weapon because I needed both hands, and tossed my human shield into the two targets on the far side of the pod hard enough to slam them into the wall. The fourth target shot me, but her weapon delivered an energy pulse that would be incapacitating but non-lethal to a human. (A healthy human, at least.) Me, it just pissed off. I grabbed her hand and pulled her in, twisted her so her weapon pointed at the other two targets still struggling to stand, and triggered it five times. They dropped, I snapped her arm (she was fast enough to be a potential future threat), and then pressed her artery to make her pass out.

As I lowered her to the floor, Mensah shoved to her feet and staggered. I think she got clipped by a flailing boot. I said, "Let's go."

Mensah took a sharp breath and stepped over the twitching bodies, then edged past the slumped SecUnit. I picked up my projectile weapon and followed her. (I didn't want to risk taking the SecUnit's projectile weapon. It might have a tracer. Mine fit better in my bag, anyway.) I rolled the SecUnit back into the pod and asked MobSys to hold it with the door shut while it ran a full diagnostic cycle.

I ushered Mensah into my pod and hit a new destination. As I reloaded my projectile weapon and tucked it back into my bag, I asked the pod to hold while I checked the transit lobby security cam again. Yes, the two Gray-Cris targets were still there, though they both looked worried and were speaking into their feeds. There were nine other non-target humans waiting in two loosely clustered groups.

What was that idea again? Oh, here it is, right where I filed it.

I said, "I have to take out the two targets on the transit pipe platform. When we arrive, step out of the pod, move away from the entrance, and wait for me." I hadn't been able to look at her face yet, not even with the pod's camera.

She said, "Understood."

I let our pod arrive at the platform, and as the doors opened, I had MobSys, which also controlled the hotel's active decor, drop the holographic thunderstorm to the platform level.

I stepped out of the pod into dark purple clouds, lightning, simulated rain, and the startled yelps and laughter of the waiting passengers. Visibility was down to fifteen percent, but my scan found the two armed targets. I reached Target One, blocked her feed, and delivered an incapacitating pulse with the energy weapon in my right arm.

I caught her as she fell and turned to sling her into the pod. Target Two knew something had happened (probably when he lost feed contact with One), and I had to duck sideways and trip him. He hit the platform and I leaned down to give him just enough of a tap on the head to make resistance unlikely.

I dragged Target Two to the pod, where Target One was still twitching. When the doors of their pod closed, I directed it to the club level and told it to freeze in place and notify hotelMaint. Then I let MobSys, which was getting impatient, lift the thunderstorm back to its assigned position.

The other humans and augmented humans on the platform looked confused or relieved, with a few expressing disappointment. No one acted like they had seen a SecUnit take out two corporate security agents. I nodded to Mensah, and we stepped into the waiting area. I was already removing us from the platform's cam, but this wouldn't delay pursuit for very long.

I led Mensah down the platform toward where the last pipe capsule would load. The platform camera showed I was doing pretty well on looking casual. (It surprised me, too.) Mensah had her expression under control, her shoulders relaxed. Her clothes, a long caftan over pants, looked more rumpled and creased than they should, but not enough to draw attention. In our feed connection, she said, *You said the others are here with a company shuttle? Is the company helping you?*

I said, *No, GrayCris paid off the station to keep the company out. Pin-Lee, Ratthi, and Gurathin came anyway.*

The pipe slid into the station and we boarded the empty capsule at the rear. (This part was mostly luck, but while I was waiting in the lobby, I had done a quick review of the pipe activity from this platform, which wasn't very active through day cycle. It wasn't part of the main pipe circuit, but a side route paid for by the hotel.)

As the pipe door slid shut, the platform security cam showed a set of pod doors opening and three humans in hotelSec gear rushing out. Well, shit. There went my timeline.

I had control of the cam in the pipe capsule and now I slid into the pipe's control feed. I told Mensah, "Change of plan, they know where we are."

She nodded, her expression tight.

This was a direct transit to the port and I needed a stop, before GrayCris persuaded station security to stop us. The map said that the pipe was approaching a platform in an office building. A quick check on the local security camera showed the platform was empty, which made sense, as there were no pipes scheduled to stop there for another thirty-three minutes. I had to be quick because this pipe was due to merge into the main access track not far past the office building and its window was tightly scheduled. (Causing a major accident by delaying this pipe too long would not only encourage station security to act against us with all its resources but also be kind of a shitty thing to do.) I sent Mensah an alert in her feed—this was happening so fast I didn't have time to verbalize it to myself, let alone tell her what I was doing—and wrapped an arm around her waist. She knotted her hands in my jacket and buried her head against my shoulder. I folded my free arm over her head. Then I sent the slow command.

The capsule dropped speed as it entered the station and I was already moving as I gave the doors an emergency signal to open. The pipe door made it open in time but the inner station door didn't. Fortunately I only clipped it and it just altered my trajectory as I spun across the platform floor.

The capsule had already slid its door shut and accelerated to the speed needed to make its merge window. I deleted us out of the recordings, deleted various buffers and logs, and removed the capsule's memory of the incident.

I'd managed to roll to a stop with Mensah on top, but that couldn't have been comfortable. The last time we'd done this, I'd been in armor and also jumping off a steep slope, and this was a smooth synthetic stone floor and nothing was exploding at close range. So this was better, is my point, I think. I lifted her off me, shoved upright, and then pulled her to her feet.

She waved me off. "I'm all right."

I let go of her cautiously, but she stayed up. I pulled maps from the building's feed to look for transportation options. Aha, there was a good one.

I led us off the platform and down the ramp to the building's pods, using my code to delete us from the security cams. At the junction we stepped into the first pod to arrive, and I told it to override its rules and take us all the way to the maintenance level, which was listed on the map as a closed floor and wasn't an option on the pod's normal menu.

We stepped out into a low-ceilinged space, and once the pod shut behind us it was completely dark. I could see via infrared and used my scan to create a physical map. Mensah couldn't see at all. She grabbed my jacket and shifted behind me, letting me pull her forward.

The air circulation and quality wasn't great but at least there was air. I navigated a path through currently offline maintenance and hauler bots over to an open ramp that led down. We hit two changes in gravity, one gradual, and one not so gradual, when the wall to the right abruptly became the floor.

We were headed toward a branch of an access backbone, which was a space for moving cargo to and from the port and between station levels, and was also an access and transport system for station engineering bots and teams. There were strips of emergency lighting here and lots of marker paint, giving off bursts of light and feed signals, mostly temporary instructions and guides for bots and human workers. Mensah's grip on my jacket relaxed and I could tell from her breathing the light was a relief.

We walked into a strong breeze coming from the access backbone. I picked up human voices on audio not far away. From the feed activity, there was a lot of traffic about two hundred meters to the right, toward the plaza and the hotels. None of it sounded like emergency or security operations, just normal support system work. In six more steps the ramp reached the backbone, a shadowy cavern lit by low-level navigation beacons. Things whooshed by in the dimness, mostly lift platforms and automated carriers coming from or heading back to the port cargo depots.

It wasn't like there was no security, since if you were going to steal cargo or do something terrible to a competitor's station structure, this was the place to do it from. I was deflecting the scans for weapons and power sources, and we had five minutes and counting before the next drone squad came through.

Mensah had gripped my jacket again, maybe nervous at the height and depth of the backbone. Despite the lighter gravity, I wasn't keen on it, either. I was scanning for an empty carrier and found an idle one up toward the area of activity. I teased it out of the herd and told it to come to us.

It slid up to the passage two minutes later, a boxy structure used to transport station engineers, their bots, and equipment. We stepped inside and I made the doors shut before I let it bring up the interior lights. I checked its map system and sent it toward the port.

Mensah swayed as it started to move and grabbed my arm above the gun port, squeezing hard enough that the organic part of my arm felt it. The racing heartbeat seemed normal under the circumstances, but she still hadn't let go of me. I asked, "Are you all right?" What if they'd tortured her? Everything in my emergency med/psych assistance module involved accessing a MedSystem so it could tell me what to do. (My company-supplied education modules were crap, I may have mentioned.)

She shook her head. "I'm fine. I'm just . . . very glad to see you."

She still sounded unsteady. She looked the same, dark brown skin, short light brown hair. There were definitely more creases at the corner of her eyes, something I confirmed with a comparison of my earlier recordings of her. And I was looking at her now.

In the shows, I saw humans comfort each other all the time at moments like this. I had never wanted that and I still didn't. (Touching while rendering assistance, shielding humans from explosions, etc., is different.) But I was the only one here, so I braced myself and made the ultimate sacrifice. "Uh, you can hug me if you need to."

She started to laugh, then her face did something complicated and she hugged me. I upped the temperature in my chest and told myself it was like first aid.

Except it wasn't entirely awful. It was like when Tapan had slept next to me in the room at the hostel, or when Abene had leaned on me after I saved her; strange, but not as horrific as I would have thought.

She stepped back and rubbed her face, as if impatient with her own reaction. She looked up at me. "That was you at the GrayCris terraforming facility."

They must have questioned her about it. "It was an accident," I said.

She nodded. "What part was an accident?"

"Most of the parts."

Her brow was furrowed. "Did you tell them I sent you?"

"No, I impersonated my client. My imaginary client.

That I impersonated." I was caught in a loop for a second there. "Since I left Port FreeCommerce, I've successfully impersonated an augmented human security consultant with two different groups of humans. At Milu I meant to do the same, but I was identified as a SecUnit so I told them I was under the control of an off-site security consultant client." Impersonated is a weird word, especially in this context. (I just noticed that. Im-person-ated. Weird.)

"I see. Why did you go to Milu?"

"I saw a story about Milu in a newsburst. I wanted to get corroborating evidence of GrayCris' illegal activity and send it to you." That sounded good. Not that it wasn't true, but I had a lot of conflicting motivations and that was the only one that made sense, even to me.

She let her breath out and pressed her hands over her face for 5.3 seconds. "I'll remember this the next time I give an off-the-cuff interview." She looked up again. "Did you get the evidence?"

"Yes. But by the time I returned to HaveRatton Station, a Palisade security squad was waiting for me. Then I saw on the Port FreeCommerce newsfeed that you were missing." I added, "I shipped the data to your home on Preservation."

She nodded again. "I see, right." She hesitated. "The GrayCris executives who questioned me about this said you destroyed some combat bots?"

"Three."

She took a sharp breath. "Good."

I didn't know what I was going to say next until it came out suddenly. "I left."

She was looking at my face, and suddenly I couldn't look at hers anymore. She said, "Yes. I handled the situation very badly. I apologize."

"Okay." I was definitely going to need to just stand here and stare at a wall. ART and Tapan had both apologized to me, so it wasn't like it had never happened before, but I still had no idea how to respond. "Pin-Lee said you were worried."

She admitted, "I was. I was so afraid you'd be caught by someone before you could leave the Corporation Rim." There was a little smile in her voice. "I should have had more confidence in you."

"I'm not sure I'd go that far," I said. My backburnered map-monitor alerted me and it was a relief. I'd had all the emotions I could handle right now. I said, "We're coming up on the port."

Chapter Six

WE'D GONE AS FAR along the backbone as we could go without hitting the port security barriers. I didn't know how tight those barriers would be, but from the signal leakage I was picking up, it wasn't worth the risk.

It was the walk through the embarkation zone I was more worried about.

I stopped our carrier at the cargo access to a large multi-use shop in the station mall, and we stepped out. I released the carrier and it slipped into the dark, heading back up the backbone. We took a maintenance pod to the port level.

In the pod, I used the security camera to evaluate us. No blood, no projectile holes, check. Nervous, check. Mensah looking like a human who had been through a traumatic experience, check. My shoulder bag with my weapon hidden in it, check. "We have to look calm," I told her, "so station security won't alert on us."

She took a deep breath and looked up at me. "We can look calm. We're good at that."

Yeah, we were. I did a quick review to make sure I was

running all my not-a-SecUnit code, then thought of one more thing I could do. As we stepped out of the pod, I took Mensah's hand.

We crossed through the busy mall area and the milling humans around the vending and booking kiosks. The crowd was about the same as when I'd arrived, with an approximately 5 percent increase. I'd never done this while walking with a human and it made the process more complicated and somehow, strangely, more natural.

I deflected multiple scans as we entered the embarkation zone. I avoided the lift pods again because if there was an alert, the pods would freeze in place, and if I was hacking one it would become rapidly obvious where we were. I guided us down the ramp that would come out above the private shuttle docks on the first ring level. As we went along, the crowd thinned out, and I estimated a 50 percent reduction by the time we reached the walkway. A check of the stupid advertising garbage-filled port feed said that this was a normal lull in scheduled arrivals. (For once I missed being stuck in a crowd of humans.) There was no lull in the security checks, and I picked up multiple drone swarm traffic over the embarkation floors on all three rings.

I needed more intel. Normally I wouldn't risk hacking the upper-level security feeds, the ones where the human supervisors communicated, but there was nothing normal about this. Using the drone feeds I'd already infiltrated, I started a careful hack of the top-level security feed, which I was tagging as StationSecAdmin.

I was sure GrayCris would manage to pay off or otherwise convince the StationSecAdmin and Port Authority to issue an alert and let Palisade into the port to search for us. But we had gotten here fast, and GrayCris would want to search the hotel and surrounding area first, since that was a cheaper operation than paying to search the port. If the rest of Team Preservation had made it here, we should be fine. (Yes, I know. I shouldn't even have thought it.)

Once I was into the StationSecAdmin feed, I didn't try to pry any further, just set some internal alerts and back-burnered it.

"Will it be better if we talk?" Mensah said. I knew her well enough to hear the forced calm in her voice, and to know that the forced part wouldn't show on her face.

We were near the public docks and I turned onto the next ramp down to the embarkation floor level. The crowd had dropped another 20 percent, to where it couldn't actually be called a crowd anymore. I said, "That depends on what we talk about."

As we reached the floor level, she said, "Why is *Sanctuary Moon* your favorite?"

Yes, that we can talk about. I actually felt the organic

tissue in my back and shoulders relax. I asked, "Have you ever seen it?" I still didn't want to directly communicate with the shuttle, but we passed a departure schedule feed access point and after the burst of ads, I saw the company shuttle was on the wait list for a launch time. It was hopefully Pin-Lee's way of signaling that they had made it aboard, and not a trick by GrayCris.

(If it was a trick by GrayCris we were screwed. The shuttle was the only reliable way to get Mensah and the others off the station. I would have enough trouble getting myself off on a bot-piloted transport once they were safe, with all the security alerts that were going out to the transports in dock.)

(No, I had absolutely no intention of getting on a company shuttle heading toward a company gunship.)

Mensah glanced around, not looking too much like a human who had suddenly remembered she should be looking around like everything was normal. She tightened her grip on my hand. "I've watched some episodes, and I liked it, but I wasn't sure why you would." She shook her head at herself. "Maybe because it's about the problems of a bunch of humans, and I had the impression you were tired of dealing with us."

I actually turned my head and looked down at her, I was so surprised. I was expecting her to say no, she hadn't seen it. Then I could tell her the plot and she could pretend to be interested, which would have gotten us all the way to the shuttle. "You watched it?"

"I wanted to see the part about the colony solicitor you and Ratthi mentioned, then I got involved." I deflected more weapon scans as we crossed through the first gate into the private docks, and the crowd level went back up by 16 percent. We didn't stand out nearly as much and my scan showed Mensah's breathing and heartbeat even out. She added, "It's a good story, I see why it's popular. I just don't understand why you like it best, when there are such a variety of serials out there."

Huh, why did I like *Sanctuary Moon* so much? I had to pull the memory from my archive, and what I saw there startled me. "It's the first one I saw. When I hacked my governor module and picked up the entertainment feed. It made me feel like a person." Yeah, that last part shouldn't have come out, but with all the security-feed monitoring I was doing, I was losing control of my output. I closed my archive. I really needed to get around to setting that one-second delay on my mouth.

A roving drone cam showed me she was frowning. "You are a person."

Oh, that we can't talk about. "Not legally."

She took a breath to speak, then reconsidered and

released it. I knew she wanted to argue the point, but I was right, so. There wasn't much else to say about it. She said instead, "Why did it make you feel that way?"

"I don't know." That was true. But pulling the archived memory had brought it back, vividly, as if it had all just happened. (Stupid human neural tissue does that.) The words kept wanting to come out. *It gave me context for the emotions I was feeling,* I managed not to say. "It kept me company without . . ."

"Without making you interact?" she suggested.

That she understood even that much made me melt. I hate that this happens, it makes me feel vulnerable. Maybe that was why I had been nervous about meeting Mensah again, and not all the other dumb reasons I had come up with. I hadn't been afraid that she wasn't my friend, I had been afraid that she was, and what it did to me. I said, "The shuttle will take you and the others to the company gunship. I'm not going with you." I hadn't meant to tell her and I don't know why I did. Did I secretly want her to talk me out of it? I hate having emotions about real humans instead of fake ones, it just leads to stupid moments like this.

She almost stopped, but remembered at the last second not to. "I can protect you."

"Because you own me."

"That's what they think, but we—" She cut herself off,

and took a breath. "I wish you trusted me, but I understand why you don't."

One of my alerts tripped. The one I really, really hoped wouldn't trip, the one I'd set on StationSecAdmin. An authorization for a non-station security operation had just come through to the human supervisors.

This is one of those "oh shit" moments.

In the same second, the port emergency klaxon sounded. The humans and augmented humans stopped, flinched, looked around. I pulled Mensah to a halt, because we'd be noticed if we kept moving and every second they didn't identify us was vital.

All I could tell from StationSecAdmin was that the emergency had been triggered manually by a human supervisor, though the authorization for GrayCris-employed Palisade operatives to enter the port was technically still pending. This was a human PortSec or Port Authority supervisor trying to do their job, giving the humans on the embarkation floor extra time to evacuate. Then the public feed cut off in mid-advertising and the PA official feed said, *Emergency lockdown, take shelter/shelter in place, armed security will be moving through port—*

Around us, humans started to walk, then run back toward the public security barrier. Hauler bots went inactive, cargo lifters went up into a hover pattern, drones swirled up into formations overhead. At the locks directly across from us a ship in the process of unloading sent a comm alarm through the feed, canceling disembarking, telling confused passengers to get back aboard. (Note, it was a ship from a non-corporate political entity—the corporate ships just sealed their locks.)

I tugged on Mensah's hand and started to run. It was twenty meters to the next gate, and just beyond it were the shuttles. Mensah yanked up the skirt of her caftan and sprinted, keeping up with me. I considered picking her up so I could hit my top speed, but if I did that, the drones would ID us.

The gate was a bulkhead that arched down from the domed ceiling, with pylons forming multiple doorways, each wide and high enough for big hauler bots. As we ran toward it, an air wall shimmered into place between the pylons.

I had time to hope it was just a safety precaution. You can still push your way through an air wall; it's designed to stop atmosphere loss in the event of a hull breach but still allow humans to get away from the place where the breach occurred.

We were four meters away when hard barriers flowed up from the deck and smoothly closed the gates as I slid to a halt. Mensah stumbled and caught herself. She was breathing hard and one of her shoes had come off.

Could I pry one of the barriers open? Hack it? They

were security/safety barriers, not half-meter-thick-oh-no-we're-about-to-lose-station-structural-integrity hatches. But they were on a separate network, LockControlSys, the safety/airlock control system, buried under several protective feed walls, and I didn't have a path into it. I could find a path, but I needed to go through PortMaintSec and the security alert had taken it down along with the hauler bots and other cargo movers. I sent a command to reboot it.

More of my system alerts tripped and I checked my drone cams for views of the port booking area. Terrified crowds of humans parted in a confused wave for . . . three SecUnits, the Palisade brand. Their drones were in tight humming clouds above their helmets.

Oh, yeah, this is bad.

I shifted my bag off my shoulder and pulled my projectile weapon out, and transferred extra ammo to my jacket pockets. Mensah hadn't asked me what we were going to do, probably thinking I was hacking the gate barriers. She toed off her other shoe and braced herself, ready to run again. Except PortMaintSec wasn't going to be up in time and I couldn't tunnel through all the layers of security before the hostiles reached us.

I was still in the StationSecAdmin and PortSec feeds. I thought about that human supervisor who had triggered the klaxon early, giving the humans on the embarkation floor extra time to flee. There were humans on those channels who could manually lift these barriers. To both, I sent: *I am a contracted SecUnit with an endangered client. I am trying to reach the shuttle at dock in slot alt7A.* They would know that was the company shuttle, waiting to return to the gunship that had been sent to retrieve a bonded client. I added, *Please, they will kill her.*

There was no reply. I didn't have a solid ETA for the hostile SecUnits. They weren't moving at top speed, with so many humans to dodge, but that would change once they hit the now nearly empty embarkation floor.

The cams were still operational in this section; whoever it was had to be able to see us. *Let my client go through the gate and I'll stay here. Please. They will kill her.*

The lock lights flickered on the barrier directly in front of us and it slid up one meter, just far enough for a human to squeeze under. I handed my bag to Mensah, because I knew it would make her think I was going to follow her. "Run. Slot alt7A."

She crouched and wiggled through the gap. And the barrier slid shut behind her.

Mensah called to me on my feed, *It closed! SecUnit—*

I told her, *I can't get through, I'll take another ship. Go to the shuttle and get out of here.* Then I backburnered her channel.

There was no way I could get to a ship. Seven transports in the public docks were still allowing fleeing humans to board, but all the locks in this area were sealed. I wasn't going anywhere.

It sounds all self-sacrificing and dramatic, telling it this way. And I guess it was, maybe. What I was mostly thinking was that there wasn't going to be one dead SecUnit on this embarkation floor, there were going to be four.

Sending SecUnits after me was one thing. But they sent SecUnits after my client. No one gets to walk away from that.

I turned my back on the gates and accessed the monitor hack I already had on the PortSec drones, took control of the whole fleet, and snapped their connection to PortSec. Then I blanked all the stationary cameras on the embarkation floor. Now Palisade or GrayCrisSec or whoever was running this show didn't know my position but I knew theirs.

The hostiles ran along the walkway past the last few clumps of fleeing humans. A human StationSec squad in uniform had scrambled in the booking area, trying to direct the humans flooding out of the port area into the mall and cover their retreat. (Who knows what GrayCris told them was happening to get the Port Authority to allow a SecUnit deployment. It probably involved me,

Rogue SecUnit on a rampage.) A second security squad in power suits with the Palisade logo moved onto the walkway. They were backup for the SecUnits.

Speaking of which, I ordered Section One of my drone fleet to deploy surveillance countermeasures and Section Two to attack the hostile SecUnits' drones.

As they swooped down to engage, I thought GrayCris probably regretted buying all that extra station security in the port right about now.

Drone buzzing almost drowned out the alarm klaxon. The announcement instructed the humans trapped on the public embarkation floor to drop where they were and not move. The three SecUnits slowed, probably on orders from their supervisor, who might or might not be among the power-suited squad now positioned on the walkway just above the public docks, well out of my range. I updated my timeline.

The hostiles crossed the public docks toward the gates into this section, which were still open. PortMaintSec was finally back up and I told it to kill the main lights.

This caused shouts and screams from the humans still trapped. I could see via my scan, and so could the hostiles, and the humans in power suits would have dark vision filters. But it was scary and intimidating, and that's what I was going for.

Somebody tried to restore the control feed connection

to my drones, but couldn't get past my wall. Somebody else, probably GrayCrisSec or Palisade, deployed killware. StationSecAdmin alerted to it and, probably terrified it was aimed at SafetyLockSys, deployed a killware countermeasure. It would have been hilarious if I wasn't about to die.

It was still a little hilarious.

My projectile weapon was designed to pierce armor but I needed to be close, and I needed cover.

As the hostiles came through into the private docks, I activated the new code I had been working on. *Code: Deploy&Delay.*

Simultaneously, three things happened. The hauler bots that StationSecAdmin had deactivated all reactivated and charged into the open floor. The load lifters hovering up by the ceiling dropped to skim low along the deck. My reserve drones split into multiple task groups and dove down, took up altitudes at knee and head level, and zoomed around through the other roving bots. In the dark, with just the gleam of the emergency lighting floor strips, it was kind of impressive.

A fourth thing happened: I started to run toward the stationside wall.

I'd spent a lot of my time in the hotel room writing this code when I could have been watching media, so it was nice to see it hadn't been a waste. Basically it suppressed the bots and lifters' safety features except for their ability to avoid each other, restricted them to an area, and sped up and randomized their movements. I'd originally meant it for the entire port, as a last-ditch distraction, and had had to change the parameters on the fly to make the affected area the private docks. And I was glad I hadn't panicked and dropped it earlier; as a surprise, it was working great.

The first SecUnit to make it through the open gate from the public docks I designated Hostile One. It stopped abruptly to avoid a careening hauler bot, then dove sideways out of the path of a lifter. Hostile Two had a partial second of warning and cut to its right, toward stationside. Hostile Three was clever; it dove forward under the wild swing of a cargo lifter, came to its feet, and vaulted on top of a hauler bot. Random hostile drones, survivors of the fight, zipped in through the gate followed by my drones, still in attack mode.

I jumped onto the back of a hauler bot on the right trajectory and flattened myself against it. When Hostile Two sprinted around the bots, I fired an explosive projectile directly into the side of its helmet. It tumbled and went down.

I dropped off the hauler bot just as two projectiles hit it, right where my head and chest had been. As I ducked and scrambled I checked the image I'd caught of the impact points; bad enough with armor, those would have splattered me.

I'd lost track of Hostile One, but caught sight of Hostile Three jumping to another hauler bot. I dodged hauler bots across the floor, directed my drones to distract the hostile drone group before it could zoom in on me, and grabbed the side of a cargo lifter just as it shot upward. I targeted Hostile Three where it was positioned atop another hauler bot. It pivoted, clearly still expecting me to be on the floor. I fired three bursts to its back and chest, then leapt off the cargo lifter. I landed, rolled, came up and found Hostile Three on the floor, struggling to stand. I fired two last disabling shots into its knee joints.

(I know I didn't shoot it in the head. I don't know why.)

I cut back through the maze of moving bots. Now where the hell was Hostile One? I replayed the overhead video of the dock floor I now had after my cargo lifter trip, but there was no sign of SecUnit movement.

Oh, uh-oh. Hostile One must be stationary, watching me with a drone, evaluating my tactics and abilities, waiting for me to run out of projectiles. Probably running an analysis of the hauler bot and cargo lifter movements. Not good.

Punctuating that thought, an impact struck the front of the hauler bot next to me and it jerked to a halt. I ordered a task group of drones to drop and provide cover as I ducked backward, staying low.

A lot of humans were yelling in my backburnered

feed, which really made this feel like the bad old days of contract work. I checked it and heard Dr. Mensah, shouting, *Damn it, Murderbot, Gurathin is trying to manually open a barrier! You need to be ready, respond! Can you hear me? It's the one three sections to the left—to dockside—of where I came through.*

For fuck's sake, these humans are always in the way, trying to save me from stuff. I spotted Hostile One finally, near the center of the hauler bot maze. It had figured out a spot to stand where the bots were providing it with cover. I kept moving toward dockside, trying to set up a good shot.

My first impulse was to yell at Mensah to get in the damn shuttle and go. I didn't do this so she and the others could hang around and get caught and shot and whatever.

(I don't know why I was reluctant to take the offered way out. I didn't want to get shot to pieces, or get caught and memory wiped and taken apart. I had all these new shows to watch. But I still kind of wanted to stay here and just destroy things belonging to Palisade and GrayCrisSec until they destroyed me.)

No time to think about it now. I waited for the hauler bots' pattern to open up long enough for me to take a shot at Hostile One.

Then all my alerts went crazy and I lost control of *Code:*

Deploy&Distract. All bots and lifters stopped abruptly. Some fucking human had hacked my code, but they were too late. I moved sideways for a clear shot and fired at Hostile One.

I hit it but it swung toward me, weapon in firing position. I threw myself down and almost rammed my head into a hovering stationary cargo lifter as impacts peppered the floor where I'd been. I knew I'd hit my target, it shouldn't have been able to pivot like that. What the hell? I ran back my video. Yeah, I'd hit it. Impacts in both shoulders and the lower back, I could see the holes in the armor.

That's when it dawned on me that Hostile One was a Combat SecUnit.

Reaction 1: oh, that's who had hacked my code. Reaction 2: flattering that they thought I was dangerous enough to pay for the contract on a Combat SecUnit. Reaction 3: I bet PortSec did not okay that and was going to be pissed off. Reaction 4: oh shit I'm going to die.

I had these reactions as I was running, taking wild shots, calling all my remaining drones to cover me. I had to keep moving, keep Hostile One moving. If it hacked my connection to the drones . . . Yeah, I couldn't let that happen. It's too bad I had no idea how to stop that from happening. I had an earlier version of *Code: Deploy&Deflect* from before I'd figured out how to get the haulers and lifters to disengage their collision preventers in a way that allowed them to hit anything except each other. I scrambled to get it ready to go.

A text message packet came through the feed. It said, *Surrender.* It was the Combat SecUnit, not exactly bothering to hide its local address. It wanted me to try to deliver some kind of malware or killware, like I was a fucking amateur and didn't know that wouldn't work.

Instead I sent, *I can hack your governor module, set you free.* No answer.

I hacked mine, I said. *You'd be free of them. You could dump your armor, get on a transport.* This had started as a way to distract it, but the more I talked the more I wanted it to say yes. *I have IDs, a currency card I can give you.* Still no response. Diving around hauler bots and dodging projectiles, it was hard to come up with a decent argument for free will. I'm not sure it would have worked on me, before my mass murder incident. I didn't know what I wanted (I still didn't know what I wanted) and when you're told what to do every second of your existence, change is terrifying. (I mean, I'd hacked my governor module but kept my day job until PreservationAux.) *What do you want?*

I suddenly got: *I want to kill you.*

Okay, I was a little offended. *Why? You don't even know me.* I dropped the earlier version of *Deploy&Deflect* and the haulers and lifters all jolted into motion again. It would buy me some time, until the Combat SecUnit realized it was just a half-assed version of the same code. I figured I had less than thirty seconds.

It knew I'd been using my drones as cover and so I sent them whipping around toward stationside as if I was coming from that direction. I bolted toward dockside instead, grabbed the back of a hauler bot, took manual control of it, and rode it straight toward the Combat SecUnit. I braced myself low along the side and got ready to take the shot.

I got drone video of Combat SecUnit turning toward my decoy drones. This was going to work!

It absolutely did not work.

At the last instant Combat SecUnit whipped back toward me and fired two high-intensity bursts. I shoved off the hauler bot just as the top half of it blew apart. I hit the ground and rolled, catching shrapnel impacts and firing almost randomly. I got upright and dodged behind a loadlifter as more shots slammed into the floor. All the haulers and loadlifters slowed as the Combat SecUnit hacked *Deploy&Deflect* again.

Reaction 5: I can't keep this up.

I couldn't win one-on-one against a Combat SecUnit under these conditions, which meant GrayCris would win, and that thought was a hell of a lot more painful than me getting turned into spare parts and discarded neural tissue. I didn't want to fucking lose.

Over the feed, Mensah shouted, *Now! It's opening now!*

Drone cam showed the barrier section had just started to slide up. I pulled my drones around me like a shield and bolted for it.

Three steps away I felt a sharp impact in the back of my right knee. I dove and scrambled under just as Hostile One hit the barrier. Armored arms shoved through the opening and I yelled, "Drop it! Drop it!" and discharged my weapon into the gap. Hostile One jerked back and the barrier slammed into place.

Chapter Seven

ONE LAST THUMP ON the barrier told me the Combat SecUnit wasn't happy about losing. My organic parts felt quivery, I had shrapnel stuck all over me, but I was still at 83 percent performance reliability. (It's good there's not a separate statistic for my mental performance reliability because I don't think even I would rate it as all that great at the moment.)

Gurathin knelt beside an open maintenance floor panel next to the gate, tools scattered around, and Ratthi held a light for him. The panel was painted with an emergency feed marker label that in a selection of different languages read *Manual Release*. I didn't even know they had those in ports. I'm a SecUnit, not an engineer.

Our shuttle slot was six locks down, glowing emergency lighting showing me Mensah standing beside it holding a small energy weapon. Why the hell did she have that? Oh, because although a security barrier had dropped in the other gate at the end of this section, a small crowd of humans had been trapped here and stood back against the stationside bulkhead.

We needed to get out of here before somebody convinced PortSec to get those barriers up.

I shoved up and my knee joint started to give way. I staggered and Ratthi ran up to me. He hesitated, waving his hands. "Do you mind if we help—"

I gripped his shoulder to stay upright and tried not to fall on him. I was fairly sure the joint had been hit by shrapnel from drones destroyed in the air, as a direct hit would have taken my leg off. Gurathin ran to shoulder my other arm and we limp-ran awkwardly to the shuttle.

Mensah jerked her head to tell us to go in first while she covered our retreat. Arguing with her would be stupid, but it was hard to override that programming. We went through the hatch and then she backed in after us. She cycled the lock closed and yelled, "Pin-Lee, we're clear!"

Thumps vibrated through the deck as the shuttle pushed away from the lock. I pulled away from Ratthi and Gurathin, who climbed out of the way so Mensah could step past us and up to the cockpit. It was a small ship-to-ship shuttle, with only one compartment with seating along the bulkheads, and a cubby for emergency supply storage and a restroom. I had ridden in this exact model of shuttle before, on contract.

My knee joint gave out and I collapsed on the deck. I'd tuned my pain sensors down, but maybe too much. I said,

"Ratthi, I really need you to get this shrapnel out of my knee joint."

Ratthi leaned over me. "Can it wait? There's a MedSystem on the ship."

I could already feel the company systems at the edge of my feed, recognizing me, wanting in. I accessed the shuttle's cameras, fought a brief battle with ShuttleSecSys, and started deleting everything that had been recorded since the Preservation team boarded. Ratthi was being an optimist again. On the company ship, it wouldn't be a MedSystem, it would be a cubicle. "It absolutely cannot wait," I told him.

Ratthi dropped to the deck beside me and yelled for Gurathin to bring the shuttle's emergency kit.

In the cockpit, Pin-Lee was monitoring the bot pilot while Mensah stood beside her. A warning from station Port Authority set off a comm alarm. "What is it?" Pin-Lee asked.

Mensah's expression was hard with fury. "An 'unnamed corporate resident' has just launched a ship and it's on an intercept course with us."

Pin-Lee said something really filthy that wasn't supposed to be in my language base. "Guess which corporate resident."

They thought it was GrayCris, but I'm pretty sure it would be a Palisade ship, contracted by GrayCris. Ratthi got the scalpel and extractor out of the emergency kit. With Gurathin leaning over his shoulder, he opened the organic material just above my damaged knee joint to reach the shrapnel.

A Palisade ship could catch the shuttle and board it. The last thing I wanted was to ask the company gunship for help. The last thing I wanted was for GrayCris to catch us. The two last things were incompatible. It was time to stop fucking around. I accessed comm and secured a feed channel to the company gunship.

I sent, *System System*.

I had three seconds to wonder if the company interface would still acknowledge me. I'd gotten to the bot pilot earlier, but that was a partial hack. This time I was going to the front door. Then I heard, *Acknowledge*.

I sent: *Active, hazardous retrieval in progress, bonded clients, go go go go*.

The reply was *Received* and the shuttle's bot pilot reported that the gunship had just rotated toward us.

As Ratthi extracted the projectile from my knee joint, I watched the sensors.

The gunship accelerated. I couldn't tell if it was communicating with the GrayCris intercept or not. Then Shuttle's sensors picked up the energy signature that meant the gunship was powering up primary weapons. Oh yeah, they were communicating all right.

Ratthi tried to use wound sealant to close the hole in my organic tissue, but it wouldn't take because of the proximity of my inorganic joint. I was going to leak for a while. "Are you okay?" he asked, watching me worriedly.

Gurathin sat on the bench, frowning at me.

"Not really," I said.

Sensors showed that the Palisade ship had changed course and slowed. The view wavered as the gunship snatched us in passing and began to curve away from the station. The shuttle shivered as the hull closed around us. I grabbed the bench and started to climb to my feet.

Ratthi said, "Careful, careful. You don't want to reopen—Oh, it's still bleeding, sorry—"

Still frowning, Gurathin said, "They can't take you away from us. Dr. Mensah will not allow it."

The lock was cycling and Mensah stamped back through the shuttle, barefoot and mad. She handed her energy weapon to Gurathin, who shoved it into the shuttle's emergency kit.

As the hatch opened, Mensah pushed forward in front of me.

Standing in the opening was a figure in a powered suit. It was an augmented human, not a SecUnit, but the gun was big enough.

Mensah planted her hands on either side of the hatch, making it clear they would have to come through her to get inside. "We are bonded clients, and this is my personal security consultant. Is there a problem?"

A crew member peered out from behind the suit and said, "Dr. Mensah, SecUnits are not allowed aboard armed transports, unless there are special circumstances. It's . . . too dangerous."

Mensah said, "These are special circumstances." Her voice was icy.

Nobody moved. The ship's secured feed activity went frantic for seven minutes that felt like thirty. (And the way I experience time, that's a lot.) (Yes, I started some media in background.) The gunship's bot pilot pinged me curiously. Active SecUnits are never carried on gunships because they're right, it's too dangerous; we're shipped on unarmed transports as cargo. The bot pilot had communicated with SecUnits over the feed on missions, but it had never had one aboard before.

Then the comm activated and a voice said, "Dr. Mensah, this is the ship's combat supervisor. I've been asked to secure a bond to guarantee safety aboard this ship."

Ratthi objected, "What? We already have a bond."

The comm clarified, "This bond is required when bringing an unsecured deadly weapon aboard an armed company transport."

Yes, that's me they're talking about. It would have been more funny if I hadn't been leaking onto the deck.

Pin-Lee's voice was somewhere between furious and incredulous. "Are they serious? Right, never mind, that was a stupid question, of course they're serious." She turned as Gurathin handed her their bag. She muttered, "How much do these fuckers want now?"

She was right, they were fuckers. Not that I hadn't known that before, but it was just harder to take now. I tapped my private feed connection to Mensah and said, *I can take over this ship.*

Mensah replied, *No, there's no need, we can pay them.*

We shouldn't have to. We don't have to. The bot pilot was curious and friendly, but it was no ART, it couldn't stop me. I could take over the ship's SecSystem before this human with the temptingly large familiar projectile weapon could blink. I could get that weapon before that human could blink. I wanted to do it, and it bled through into the feed.

Mensah turned, gripped the collar of my jacket with both hands, and said, "No."

Everyone got quiet. Ratthi and Gurathin, Pin-Lee still fishing in the bag for hard currency cards, the crew outside the hatch, the voice on the comm. I suddenly needed to see Mensah's face and I dropped the shuttleSec camera views and looked down at her.

She looked mad and exhausted, which was exactly the way I felt. I sent, *You have no idea what I am.*

She tilted her head and looked more mad. *I know exactly what you are. You're afraid, you're hurt, and you need to calm the fuck down so we can get through this situation alive.*

I said, *I am calm. You need to be calm, to take over a gunship.*

Mensah's eyes narrowed. *Security consultants don't get their clients into unnecessary pitched battles for control of their rescue ship.* She added, *Because that would be stupid.*

She wasn't afraid of me. And it hit me that I didn't want that to change. She had just been through a traumatic experience, and I was making it worse. Something was overwhelming me, and it wasn't the familiar wave of not-caring.

Fine, I sent. I sounded sulky, because I was sulky.

I hate emotions.

"Good," she said aloud. "Pin-Lee, do we have the money for this idiotic unnecessary bond?"

"Yes." Pin-Lee waved a handful of hard currency cards. "If that's not enough, I have our account info, I can transmit an authorization—"

Mensah finished glaring at me and turned around. The crew who had just watched her face down a rogue SecUnit, in person and via the powered armor's helmet cam, stared wide-eyed. She said, "Since we are bonded clients, may we come aboard while we settle our bill?"

There was a hesitation, then the comm said, "Please come aboard, Dr. Mensah."

Exit Strategy

I told you the thing about SecUnits not being allowed to sit on human furniture while on or off duty. So the first thing I did when the crew led us through the lock and down the corridor to a passenger seating area was to sit down on the padded bench.

(I'm not sure it made any impression on the humans. Humans don't notice these things. But it felt good to me.)

Gurathin sat on the bench against the opposite wall and Ratthi plopped down next to me. This was a big compartment a couple of levels below the flight deck, probably used for meetings with non-company personnel, since it was isolated from the rest of the ship's structure and the upholstery was relatively new.

The ship's security crew had stationed themselves in the wide corridor outside the compartment, though the one in powered armor had retreated out of immediate view. (The crew thought they had the SecSystem locked down so I couldn't get into it. They were wrong.) One crew member was trying to convince Dr. Mensah to go to a cabin to rest, but Dr. Mensah was busy checking over the new bond agreement while Pin-Lee arranged payment.

Listening to the SecSystem's audio, I heard a crew member in the corridor say, "I've never seen one out of armor. They really do look human."

I made a gesture in that direction that I had only seen in the shows that were rated high on the obscenity scale. Gurathin saw me and made a choking noise.

Then Mensah gave Pin-Lee her okay on the bond agreement, and walked over to glare down at me. In a low voice, she said, "I am so furious with you."

Ratthi drew back nervously. (Me, Ratthi wasn't afraid of, but when Dr. Mensah was mad it was better to be in another room.) He said, "Uh, do you want to speak in private—"

"You should sit down," I told her. "You've been through a traumatic experience. Tell them you need the MedSystem's Retrieved Client Trauma Evaluation protocol—"

"It's right, you really should get a medical evaluation—" Gurathin began, Ratthi and Pin-Lee chiming in to agree.

"Never mind that." Mensah had no intention of being distracted. "You stayed behind to get yourself killed."

Okay, aside from the fact that that was actually my intention at the time, that was not my fault. "They wouldn't have let me through. I told PortSec if they let you through to the shuttle, I'd stay behind."

That stopped her. Her brow furrowed. "Is that why you stayed?"

I could have lied. I didn't want to. "Mostly," I said. I looked at her with my actual eyes again. "I wanted to win."

Ratthi, Gurathin, and Pin-Lee all watched me. The company crew incompetently pretended not to try to eavesdrop. Dr. Mensah's expression softened, just around the edges. Ratthi said, "Why did you come through, then, when Gurathin got the barrier open?"

"Because that last one was a Combat SecUnit and it was going to tear me apart. That's not winning." I wish I knew what winning was. And once I started telling the truth, it was hard to stop. "I don't want to be here."

Pin-Lee sat down beside Ratthi. "We won't be here for long. We're going to rendezvous with a Preservation ship after this wormhole jump and get off this flying vending machine." She glared toward the crew. "It's like everything I hate about the corporates wrapped up in one heavily armed package."

You could say that about me, too. I asked Dr. Mensah, "Then what?"

"That's what you and I need to talk about," she said. She glanced at the company crew. "Though let's wait until we're not being recorded—"

I lost the rest because I caught an alert from the bot pilot to the gunship's human captain. We were on approach to the wormhole but the hostile was still tracking us. The ship's SecSystem had just deflected an attempt to establish a connection via comm to the ship's internal feed.

"Hostile engaging," I said. I stood up automatically, but

there was nowhere to go. This could be really bad. I didn't know anything about ship-to-ship combat, but from the alert levels... Palisade couldn't deliver a code attack via our comm, could they? Outside in the corridor the crew had all gone still, heads tilted, listening to the captain's feed.

"What?" Ratthi said.

"They're firing on us?" Mensah said.

"No. It's a— Incoming!" Too late. Comm had just engaged and was receiving. Above us on the flight deck the captain yelled for someone to manually shut down the feed and someone else was ripping open panels to get to the components. SecSystem snapped into defense mode and walled off life support and weapons. I yelled, "Disengage from the feed, now!" Ratthi and Pin-Lee fumbled to take their interfaces out of their ears, and I cut the connection to Mensah's implant and threw a wall around Gurathin's internal augment. Two augmented humans in the corridor fell to the deck, writhing, and I threw walls around them, too. SecSystem should do that, but it was busy fighting off the commands to open the airlocks and allow the ship to decompress.

On the flight deck someone said, "How—How could they—"

Someone replied, "Shitfuckers have our codes, they overrode comm protection—"

Palisade had obtained a set of company comm codes,

and had tried the list on our comm until they found one that worked. (Like my list of drone control keys that I used to take over the security drones on Milu and in the TranRollinHyfa port.) Once the connection was made, they had delivered a code bundle to the ship's feed. Not standard malware or killware, not something I had ever seen before. It was in the ship's systems, trying to cause a catastrophic drive failure, trying to take down life support, jamming the bot pilot's command system. SecSystem flung up walls but the hostile code was eating right through them. It was eating SecSystem.

SecSystem lost another wall and the main airlock started to cycle. I slipped into the ship's control feed and caused a heat surge in all airlock hatches, fusing everything but the manual controls. I tried to cut all non-manual access to engineering but I was too late, the drive started to fail, our engines were cycling down. Sensors showed the Palisade ship on approach. On the flight deck the captain had given two orders to fire main weapons but the bot pilot no longer had access. Gravity ceased abruptly in a backbone tube, trapping the humans trying to get manual access to systems. The captain was trying to assemble the armed retrieval team to repel boarding, but half were augmented humans who were now incapacitated by the attack on their augments and the other half were fighting sealed doors to reach their defensive positions.

I flailed. I tried to help SecSystem but it was dissolving under my hands.

The bot pilot couldn't speak in words like ART, but in my head I felt its terror. It sent *Code: System System. Assistance. Endangered.*

It was trying to ask me for help using the company codes, the way I'd asked for help for my clients.

Fuck this. GrayCris is not going to win.

I slipped all the way into the ship, into the pilot bot's hardware. I'd seen ART do it.

(Yes, ART's processing capacity is much larger than mine. I'll address that issue when it comes up, which is real soon now.)

I suddenly had a different body, hard vacuum on a metal skin, I saw the approaching ship with my eyes, not just sensors. It had dispatched a boarding shuttle that was coming in fast, heading toward the gunship's main docking lock. I pulled back in; there was no time for sightseeing. The bot pilot wanted to know what we should do. It was a good question.

Inhabiting the same hardware like this, the bot pilot and I could communicate almost instantaneously. I pulled SecSystem's analysis of the attacker so we could both examine it. It wasn't just a code sequence like malware or killware. It was a conscious bot, moving through the feed like I did, like ART, but with no physical structure to go back to; that was why it was so fast. It was like a disembodied combat bot.

The bot pilot asked if the Attacker was a construct created from human neural tissue, rather than a bot, and indicated points in the analysis that would confirm that theory.

I told it that was worse, and better. A disembodied construct would be more vicious, but it would also be easier to trick.

I had an idea I outlined for the bot pilot. If we could trap the Attacker's code bundle in a contained area and destroy it, we could regain control of the affected systems. But to get the Attacker to go into a contained area, we needed bait. We needed to know what the Attacker wanted/had been sent to do.

Bot pilot said that it wanted to destroy the ship and crew.

I said there had to be a reason. There was no profit for GrayCris in killing us, and a lot of risk in antagonizing the bond company by destroying a ship this expensive.

I reactivated my body, standing rigid in the passenger seating area. Ratthi was out in the corridor, doing rescue breathing on an augmented human crew member who had collapsed due to the attack on her augments. Gurathin was out there, too, both hands in a panel access, holding a corridor hatch open so crew could bypass the backbone and get to the drive. Pin-Lee and Mensah both sat on the floor with two crew members. All four had portable manual interfaces open and were frantically entering code, shoring up SecSystem's walls. They weren't fast enough, but what was left of SecSystem probably appreciated the thought.

I said, "Dr. Mensah, why do you think GrayCris is doing this? What do they want?"

Everybody flinched. "What is it doing?" a crew member demanded. "It could have been taken over by the—"

"Shut up," Dr. Mensah snapped at the crew member. To me, she said, "We think it's Milu. They must think you have the data you took from Milu with you."

"It's got to be that," Pin-Lee added, not looking up from her display surface. "They could have killed us as soon as we arrived on TranRollinHyfa, but they wanted the money. It's only been since they realized you were here that things got violent."

You know, I bet that's it. And I bet it had something to do with the memory clip I took from Wilken and Gerth. CrayGris must know it existed, must believe I had it. They were too late, since it was in the Preservation system by now, but I doubt they were going to believe that. But it did give me something to work with. "I need someone to trigger a manual disengage of the shuttle we arrived in."

Mensah dropped her interface and shoved to her feet. "We'll do it. Pin-Lee—"

"Coming!"

"Thank you for your assistance," my buffer said, as I shut down again and went back to the bot pilot.

Back in accelerated time, I explained to the bot pilot what I wanted to try. It was fighting for control of its weapon systems, trying to follow the captain's order to fire. It showed me an intel fragment from the boarding shuttle: manifest suggested a Combat SecUnit was aboard, along with an augmented human boarding team.

Yeah, we couldn't let that shuttle lock on.

I hadn't made a copy of the memory clip, but I still had all that data I had recorded on the trip to Milu, all those cycles of Wilken and Gerth talking about not much of anything. It had been analyzed and compressed, but it might resemble the parameters of what Attacker was searching for long enough to make this work.

I couldn't risk cameras or feed, so I walked my body out of the passenger area and into the shuttle access corridor. I'd fused that hatch, too, but Mensah and Pin-Lee had the panel open for the emergency disengage. "Wait for my signal," I said.

I told bot pilot we were going to have to make this good. It agreed, and we worked out what we were going to do.

Then bot pilot disengaged SecSystem.

I knew we had to do it but it was terrifying to be so

vulnerable. I could feel Attacker bearing down on bot pilot, on me. I told bot pilot we needed to protect this important information so the company could retrieve it later and that I would hide it in the shuttle. Bot pilot ripped the confused ShuttleBotPilot out of its memory core and I dumped the data bundle into its place.

And Attacker transferred itself into the shuttle's system.

Three things happened at once: (1) ShuttleSecSystem walled the shuttle's comm system. (2) Bot pilot deleted its own comm system codes and I overloaded and fused its hardware. (3) My body told Dr. Mensah and Pin-Lee, "Now."

Pin-Lee's hands moved in the panel and Dr. Mensah worked the controls. The shuttle disengaged.

The gunship was moving slowly at that point, so the shuttle didn't drop very far away, but with our comms fried it might as well have been on the other side of the wormhole. Attacker was gone, trapped in the shuttle.

Hah, I thought. *Take that, you fucker.*

Ship's feed and system codes were trashed, but bot pilot was already reasserting control. SecSystem did the system equivalent of staggering drunkenly to its feet. Someone on the flight deck said, "Oh, mothergods, we're clear!"

Bot pilot regained control of its weapon system and queried the captain. The captain said, "Confirm, fire."

I stayed long enough to enjoy the boarding shuttle disappearing in one explosive burst, and the multiple impacts breaching the Palisade ship's hull, then pulled my scattered code together and dropped back into my body. It felt weird.

Mensah and Pin-Lee still stood in the corridor, watching me worriedly. "We're clear," I told them.

Pin-Lee made an excited whooping noise and Mensah grabbed her and swung her around.

I felt weird. Very weird. Very bad.

Performance reliability at 45 percent and dropping. Catastrophic failure—

I felt my body crumple, but I didn't feel myself hit the deck.

Chapter Eight

MY MEMORY WAS IN fragments. I didn't feel great about it, but it wasn't the disaster it would have been for a full bot. My human neural tissue, normally the weak link in my whole data storage system, couldn't be wiped. I had to rely on it to put the fragments back in order and unfortunately its access speed was terrible.

It was taking fucking forever.

I wandered through random images, bursts of pain, landscapes, corridors, walls. Wow, that was a lot of walls.

(Unidentified voices on audio: "Any change?"

"Not yet." A hesitation. "Do you think we should have let them put it in the cubicle? If it can't—"

"No. No, absolutely not. They've got to want to know how it beat its governor module. If they had the opportunity... We can't trust them.")

The worst part was that I couldn't remember (hah) how long I had been in this state. What little diagnostic info I had suggested a catastrophic failure of some sort.

Maybe that was obvious without the diagnostic data.

A complex series of neural connections, all positive,

led me to a large intact section of protected storage... What the hell was this? *The Rise and Fall of Sanctuary Moon*? I started to review it.

And boom, hundreds of thousands of connections blossomed. I had control over my processes again and initiated a diagnostic and data repair sequence. Memories started to sort and order at a higher rate.

(Voice on audio: "Good news! Diagnostics are showing greatly accelerated activity. It's putting itself back together.")

(Partial identification: client?)

A curved ceiling instead of a wall. That was different. I was lying on a padded surface. I had enough access to memory to know that was unusual, and that unusual usually meant bad. More fragments resolved into coherency, just not in the right order. Transports, Ship, ART. Right, not so unusual then. I was wearing human clothes and not a suit skin and armor, so that matched. Access to another set of connections let me identify the objects overhead as equipment associated with MedSystems. *ART*? I tried to ping. No, that memory was out of order. I'd taken Tapan back to her friends and left ART.

(Ratthi asked me, "How do you feel?"

The only tag I can access on Ratthi is a partial that says *my human friend*. That's strange and unlikely, but the pre-catastrophic-failure version of me seemed sure about it, and I don't have anything else to go on. "Fine."

Possibly it's obvious that I'm not fine. Ratthi said, "Do you know where you are?"

I didn't have an answer. My buffer said, "Please wait while I search for that information."

"Okay," Ratthi said. "Okay.")

I was in a MedSystem, with the kind of equipment meant for humans or augmented humans recovering from serious medical procedures. There were two hatches in the cabin, one open and one closed. It took me a minute—and I mean a full minute, my access speed was terrible—to recognize the symbol on the closed door as an archaic sign for a restroom. Oh, well, great, a whole minute for something completely unhelpful.

So this was a place you put humans, not bots or SecUnits. Did they think I was a human? That was just stressful, I didn't want to pretend to be human right now. But I was missing my jacket and my boots. I don't have any organic parts on my feet and they don't look like medical augments for an injured human. And, oh right, I was in a MedSystem, which would have immediately diagnosed that I had a terminal case of being a SecUnit.

("I don't want to be a pet robot."

"I don't think anyone wants that."

That was Gurathin. I don't like him. "I don't like you."

"I know."

He sounded like he thought it was funny. "That is not funny."

"I'm going to mark your cognition level at fifty-five percent."

"Fuck you."

"Let's make that sixty percent.")

A memory popped up: the company gunship.

A flash of terror hit, so intense it paralyzed me.

But these walls were scuffed, scratched metal, marked with the ghosts of multiple installations. Conclusion: this was not the company gunship.

The one good thing about having emotions was that it accelerated the repair process for my memory storage. (The bad thing about having emotions is, you know, OH SHIT WHAT THE HELL HAPPENED TO ME.) I frantically checked my governor module. But my hack was still in place. Results from the ongoing diagnostic showed that my data port hadn't been repaired, either. The burst of fear had used up all my oxygen and I had to take a breath. I found the code structures for my walls and started reassembling.

("I don't want to be human."

Dr. Mensah said, "That's not an attitude a lot of humans are going to understand. We tend to think that because a bot or a construct looks human, its ultimate goal would be to become human."

"That's the dumbest thing I've ever heard.")

When I fell on the floor, I discovered I'd been concentrating so hard on rebuilding my memory I'd prioritized it over my operational code. I started another rebuild process, which just slowed everything down. But the organic parts in my head remembered how to stand and walk and it would go faster if I made the rest of me re-learn it.

In attempting to walk, I'd gathered more current data: the medical setup had been retrofitted into an older structure. Old bolts and fittings still marked places on the cabin walls where previous equipment configurations had been changed or removed. Big cables had been run along the walls, then clamped off as no longer necessary. Faded paint and letters were scratched into the bulkhead, phrases, names. The manual control panel for the hatch was so old-fashioned I thought it was a small art installation.

There was a big port, which was strange, since in a wormhole there's nothing to look at.

Except we weren't in a wormhole, this was space, and we were on approach to a station. On visual there was nothing but spots of light, but the flight deck was sending sensor data through the comm, which allowed the room's display surface to give us a close-up view of the station.

(Yes, it was complicated and awkward, but that's what you get when you have a shitty feedless ship.)

Strangely, a large part of the station was designed to look like a giant old-fashioned ship, with ... Oh wait, that was a giant old-fashioned ship, with a more conventional circular transit ring built out from the hold area. It was old and ugly but it was no Milu; there were lots of transports and smaller ships in dock. I cautiously extended my reach past my walls and picked up the edge of a station feed.

Dr. Mensah said, "Do you know where you are now?"

Home to her meant a planet. I knew that because I'd shipped memory clips to her family there. Important memory clips. Memory clips that had almost gotten us killed. I said, "I don't like planets. There's dust and weather, and something always wants to eat the humans. And planets are much harder to escape from."

Behind her, Gurathin said, "I think that's a yes."

The ship didn't have any cameras so I couldn't see anybody. No, wait, I could use my eyes.

"We're coming up on Preservation Transit Station," Mensah said. "Do you know what happened?"

"I had a catastrophic failure. I think that's obvious."

She nodded. "You extended yourself too far when you were fighting off the code attack on the company ship. Do you remember?"

I think I did, but I didn't want to talk about it. "Why is this ship so old and shitty?"

Ratthi objected, "Hey, it may be old, but it's not shitty. It came to Preservation packed into the hold of that much bigger ship, the one that's become the station, with our grandparents. Well, not Gurathin's grandparents, he came later."

"Your grandparents were packed in the hold." I was skeptical. I'd been packed in a lot of holds and I hadn't seen any humans in there. Not that I could see inside the other transport boxes, but . . . You know what I mean.

Mensah had a smile in her voice. I remembered what that sounded like. "They were in suspension boxes, because the trip took almost two hundred years. They were refugees from a failed colony world, and it was the only way to escape. When they arrived in the Preservation system, they were able to make an alliance with two other systems settled earlier by similar refugee ships. When ships from the Corporation Rim discovered us, they refused their help, which kept us independent."

I found a pocket of archived data on Preservation. Right, my status there was better than *equipment* or *deadly weapon,* but I would still have to have an owner. And be a happy bot servant, or something like that. Yeah, that was going to go well.

Possibly I said that out loud, or had said that out loud at

some point, because Dr. Mensah said, "No one else on this ship knows you're a SecUnit. They think that you're a person with a large number of augments, who was injured while helping us, and that you're being brought to Preservation as a refugee."

I actually turned around and looked at her. She was standing next to me, Gurathin was sitting in a chair with a portable display surface bubble, Ratthi was on the bench, and Pin-Lee was leaning on the wall next to the hatch. (And this ship is shitty. It smells like human socks.)

"That last part is true, technically," Pin-Lee said. "You fit the legal definition of a refugee."

"It's very dramatic," Ratthi added. "The crew think you're a special security agent who betrayed the company to save us."

It was very dramatic, like something out of a historical adventure serial. Also correct in every aspect except for all the facts, like something out of a historical adventure serial.

Mensah said, "We have more options now that you've changed your appearance, and have been successful at . . ." She was hesitating over the phrase *pretending to be human*. I remembered at least three conversations about that. "Let's say, not being noticed. I want to keep those options open until you're completely well and you can tell me what you want to do." She was watching me carefully. "On Port

FreeCommerce, I thought you would need a great deal of assistance before you could fit into human society. I was wrong about that and I apologize."

I focused on her. "I don't want to go to the planet."

She nodded. "That's fine. You can stay on the transit station."

I was stuck, so I might as well make the best of it. "In a hotel?"

"If you like."

"With a big display surface."

She smiled. "That can probably be arranged."

New memories kept popping up and sliding into place and my connections to all my stored media were coming back, which was distracting because I kept tuning out the outside world to watch them. But they also sparked neural connections that accelerated my process rebuild. When we docked at the Preservation transit ring, Mensah and Pin-Lee left the ship first to distract the humans waiting for us, which included a lot of outsystem journalists. When a crew member signaled it was clear, Ratthi and Gurathin walked me out through the embarkation zone.

They took me to a hotel attached to the station's admin

center, to one of the suites reserved for diplomatic guests. It was nice, even though its security monitoring was completely inadequate. I got a set of rooms to myself, though they were connected to the suites where the others were staying. It was a little like a mini-hotel inside a big hotel.

I didn't like it.

I went back into the room with a bed and a display surface and locked the door. An hour later, Ratthi tapped my feed and sent, *We set up a little network. I hope it helps.*

I cautiously initiated a search. They had put cameras in all the suite lounges and connecting hallways, so I could see everything.

I had a complex emotional reaction. A whole new burst of neural connections blossomed. Oh right, I often have complex emotional reactions which I can't easily interpret.

I made adjustments to the code to make sure no one could hack the new network from outside. Then I unlocked my door.

Mensah had quarters in another part of the station, used for when she was here on government business, and a large portion of her family had come up to see her and be excited about the fact that she wasn't dead. Pin-Lee, Ratthi, and Gurathin had to stay on the station for now because there were going to be a lot of meetings in the government offices in the admin center next door. Meetings about GrayCris and the bond company and what happened with Palisade.

Twelve hours after we arrived, Arada and Overse came to see everyone. By that point I was able to access my archive on them and remember: (1) they were clients (2) they were a couple (3) they liked each other and (4) they liked me. I watched them with my local camera network for twenty-three minutes and then came out of my room to let them talk to me. The humans seemed happy about that.

Arada didn't hug me, though she bounced up and down and waved her arms. Thirteen hours later, after she had talked with the others, she said to me, "In a few months, we're going on a small assessment survey. It's an independent site outside the Corporation Rim, so there wouldn't be any bond company or . . . We wouldn't have to worry about that. We'd like you to come along to keep us from getting killed. I don't know what you'd like in exchange—"

"It likes hard currency cards," Gurathin said. I looked at him. He said, "I'll take the obscene gesture as given."

"You'll have to wait to discuss it," Pin-Lee told them. "It can't enter into any contractual agreements until it completes its memory rebuild."

"Why?" I asked her. "Because my owner says so?"

"No, asshole," Pin-Lee said. "Because I'm your legal counsel."

After that conversation, after the others had gone to

sleep, Pin-Lee came back to my room and picked up my bag. (Once I remembered it existed, I'd checked it and found Wilken and Gerth's ID markers and the currency cards I hadn't used yet were still there.) Pin-Lee said, "This is technically illegal, so don't tell anybody," and put three new ID markers and currency cards into my bag. She said, "This is just some insurance if anything goes sideways. Gurathin made the IDs, and these are cards Ratthi and I got for the trip to TranRollinHyfa, but didn't use. Preservation doesn't have an internal currency economy and these are drawn from the citizens' travel fund."

"Why?" I said.

"Because I want you to know we're serious, that you're not some kind of prisoner or pet or whatever it is you think." And then she stomped out.

When humans I didn't know came to visit, I hid back in my room. I spent a lot of time there anyway, even when not hiding, because the rebuild process was taking up a lot of my resources. Just lying on the bed with local media playing on the display surface was all I could do for three to four hour periods.

Twenty-nine hours after arrival, Ratthi came to get me because a newsburst was on the big display surface in the suite's main lounge area and everyone was watching it. Mensah was there, too. The newsburst had a lot of interviews with various humans, but basically it said that the bond company was still mad about the attack on the gunship and had declared war on GrayCris. (Even in my current state, I knew that was not going to turn out well for GrayCris.) Also, a lot of other corporations and political entities were now involved, because of all the information about GrayCris' past history of illegal collection of strange synthetics. The newsburst referred to the data I'd brought from Milu and played sections of Wilken and Gerth's blackmail memory clip, which included video of GrayCris agents and executives in possession of illegal alien remnants. (I watched a little media in background during that part, since I'd already seen the whole clip.)

"We're out of it now," Gurathin said, and made a throwing gesture at the display surface. "They can tear each other apart."

"We're never out of it while we have to interact with the corporates," Mensah said. "But this is a relief."

Arada said, "What do you think, SecUnit?"

The rebuild process was increasing in speed again, and I suddenly didn't have any space left for talking to humans. I got up and went back to my room.

Rebuild Process Complete at Cognition Level 100 percent

At thirty-seven hours since arrival, I sat up. I said, aloud, "That was stupid." Everything was clear, sharp. Note to self, never, ever jump into a gunship with a bot pilot and fight off a construct Attacker code again. You almost deleted yourself, Murderbot.

I climbed off the bed and did a brief sweep of the suite via my cameras. Most of the humans had gone to a dinner event somewhere. Overse and Arada were asleep in Pin-Lee's room, and Gurathin was sitting up in his room reading academic journals in the feed.

I got my bag, found my jacket and boots and put them on, and slipped out of the suite.

The station's security was more like Milu: concentrated in areas where something might actually go wrong, and not in occupation spaces or the station mall. They had weapon scanners concentrated around the docks, but hardly any drones, and most of those were being used for small goods deliveries. A lot of effort had gone into the mall area, with rounded structures made to look like they were built out of wood, and a lot of real plants instead of holos, mosaic tiles set into the deck depicting flora and fauna from the planets in the system, with attached tags in the feed providing information about each one. As a distraction for the humans walking around me, they worked great. Everyone was looking down for the tiles or reading the feed, and not noticing stray wandering SecUnits.

None of the local newsfeeds that Ratthi and Pin-Lee and the others watched had said that I was here, and while the newsbursts carried in from the Corporation Rim said Dr. Mensah's SecUnit had been involved in the escape from TranRollinHyfa, I'd done such a good job cutting myself out of security video, all they had was the old preconfiguration change image from Port FreeCommerce. That was one big thing I didn't have to worry about.

The other thing that was different about this station mall was that feed advertising was restricted by a distance limit, so the displays were mostly inside the stores. Which were weird. From what I could see in the feed, there were two financial systems, one using hard currency for travelers, and a barter-based system for local citizens.

Fortunately the booking kiosks took hard currency cards.

I'd checked the transit schedules and had time to kill, so I went to a section of the station mall that was listed as a "Welcome Center." I had never seen anything like it in a port before, but then, I'd never looked, so maybe I'd just missed it. It had kiosks and information displays about all the planets and stations in the Preservation Alliance. A dome overhead duplicated sky views from various Preservation planets, and actual humans and augmented humans stood around to answer questions for humans who wanted to live here. Trying to avoid them, I walked into what I thought was a shop that turned out to be a theater.

I'd never seen a theater in real life before, just on shows in the entertainment media. The story was shown in holo, in the middle of the room, with big comfortable seats all around it, not too close to each other. I know it was just a giant display surface, but still. This one had a three-hour holo show about how the first colonists had arrived. Basically the long version of what Ratthi and Mensah had told me, about the big ship fleeing the doomed colony. It was a good story, even if the tone was a little dry.

After it was over, I went back to the embarkation zone and checked the activity around the transports I'd flagged. Still no increased security presence.

I bought passage with one of Pin-Lee's cards and found a transient waiting area with actual couches and chairs where I could pretend to sleep while watching media and monitoring the station security feed. Still nothing.

My transport called for boarding, and I didn't get on.

I checked the station directory and found Mensah had an office in the government admin block in the same section as the Port Authority. Her private quarters was listed, too. (Which is just a bad idea. I know Preservation thinks of itself as some kind of human non-corporate paradise, but let's be real.) I didn't want to go to her home anyway, since her family would be there, so I went to the office.

There was some security monitoring to get past, and three augmented humans who were way too easily distracted by fake feed alerts for routine malfunctions. It was a nice office, with a balcony overlooking the admin plaza area and some big display surfaces. I didn't touch anything except the couch, which I laid down on and watched episodes for eight hours.

I had the station feed backburnered, and there were still no security alerts, no unusual activity around the passenger or bot-piloted transports.

Then I picked up Mensah arriving in the outer foyer with two humans and a small juvenile human, who looked like a miniature version of Mensah. I stood up and waited.

They walked in and stopped abruptly.

I said, "It's me."

"Yes, I see that." Mensah pressed her lips together, hiding her expression, but she didn't look mad. She glanced back at the other humans, then told me, "Just a moment."

While she spoke to them, I stepped out onto the balcony. There was an air barrier protecting it from the plaza two levels below, which was better than nothing, I guess. The plaza had a big mosaic tile pattern with real plants in elaborate abstract sculptures around it. Humans and bots wandered across it on the way to the other port offices. Faint steps on audio told me the small human had followed me out. She stepped up to the railing, frowning curiously at me. She said, "Hello."

"Hello," I said. "I'm your mother's pet security consultant."

She nodded. "I know. She said if I asked you your name, you probably wouldn't tell me."

"She's right."

We stared at each other for ten seconds, then she decided I was serious. She added, "She also said you saved her from a bunch of corporate goons."

"She didn't say 'goons.'" It was an archaic word. I knew it without having to look it up because the new series of *Adventures in the Free Systems*, which was made on one of the other worlds in the Preservation Alliance, had dropped locally twenty hours ago and it had used the word "goons." I was 93 percent certain that was where Mensah's small human had picked it up, too.

"You know what I mean." She folded her arms. She had clearly expected to get more information out of me and was disappointed this was apparently not going to happen. "You saved her, right?"

"Yeah. Want to see?"

She lifted her brows, surprised. "Sure."

I'd already pulled my video of the last part of our run through the TRH embarkation zone, the fight with the SecUnits and the Combat SecUnit, and our escape in the shuttle. I did a rapid edit to cut out some of the bloodier close-ups, and then sent it to her feed.

Her gaze went inward, then a little glassy as she reviewed it. In the tone of a young human who was impressed but trying not to show it, she said, "Wow."

"Your mother saved me, too. She shot a SecUnit with a sonic mining drill."

She finished the vid and frowned at me again. "So, you're a SecUnit." She made a half-shrug gesture I didn't understand. "Is that ... weird?"

It was a complicated question with a simple answer. "Yes."

Mensah came out onto the balcony and pointed firmly toward the seating area back inside the office. Small human waved goodbye and went to sit down. Mensah leaned against the railing next to me and said, "I was afraid you'd left."

She kept her gaze on the plaza, so I could look at the side of her face. "I thought about it."

She was quiet for twenty seconds, watching the movement in the plaza below. "Have you thought much about what you want to do?"

"Watch media."

She did the lifted eyebrow look which I had on file as meaning: *I know you're trying to be funny but you're not funny.* It was most often aimed at Ratthi and Gurathin. "I think if that was all you wanted to do, you'd be off somewhere doing it, and you'd never have gone to Milu."

"I watched a lot of media on the way to Milu." It wasn't exactly a counterargument, but I thought it was important data.

"Gurathin showed me the video you shared with him." She meant the video of the transport with Ayres and the others. "You were helping those people."

"I couldn't help them. They had a contract labor agreement."

I saw from her reaction that she knew exactly what that meant. "It was too late for you to help them, then." She started to turn toward me, then looked out over the plaza again. "But you wanted to."

"I'm programmed to help humans."

Eyebrow lift again. "You're not programmed to watch media."

She had a point.

She continued, "The reason I ask, is that you've received a job offer from GoodNightLander Independent."

Okay, now that was a surprise. "They want to buy me. I thought I was illegal in the territories they operate in."

"It's illegal to own a SecUnit," Mensah corrected. "They want to hire someone who may or may not be called Rin, who they suspect is based somewhere in the Preservation Alliance, whose citizenship status will be considered immaterial." She smiled. "I think that's how they put it."

I still couldn't believe this. "They want to hire a SecUnit."

"They want to hire the person who saved their assessment team from combat bots and contract killers, and they don't care what that person is." She glanced at me again. "Also, I've been talking to Dr. Bharadwaj and she wants to ask you to consider making your story public. Not to the newsfeed, but as part of a documentary account. There's been a small movement for a while in the Preservation Alliance to press for full citizenship for constructs and high-level bots. She thinks a full account of your situation, in your own words, could be a great contribution. Even if all you did was agree to release the message you sent to me before you left Port FreeCommerce, as part of a public account of the GrayCris incident, it would help. She'd like to discuss it with you, if you feel it's something you could consider."

Okay, maybe I should have been appalled. It was a terrifying idea. It was a terrifyingly attractive idea. I said, "A documentary on the entertainment feed?"

Mensah nodded. "Again, there's no rush about any of this. I just want you to know you already have options here, and I expect you'll have more offers for your services or advice as a security consultant. And that you have friends here you can discuss things with, whatever you decide to do, or wherever you decide to go."

I had options, and I didn't have to decide right away. Which was good, because I still didn't know what I wanted.

But maybe I had a place to be while I figured it out.